Book of Fantasies
White

K.

Copy Editor: Elizabeth M. Johnson
Book Cover Art: Cora Graphics

ISBN-10: 0615971660
ISBN-13: 978-0615971667 K World Ventures

DEDICATION

This first book is dedicated to my Nana. I finally found the courage to get out of my own way to fulfill the dream we talked about many years ago.

By K

Book of Fantasies Trilogy

Coming Soon!

Red – Book II

Black – Book III

CONTENTS

ACKNOWLEDGMENTS

This book would not have been possible without the support and patience of my family – you are my life. Deepest gratitude goes out to my significant other. Without you my life would be incomplete. I would like to take this opportunity to express gratitude to the people who have been instrumental in the successful completion of this book. Finally, an honorable mention goes out to those literary inspirations that teach and write about the Law of Attraction. Without you, this book trilogy would have remained only a dream.

INTRODUCTION

Fantasy is described as an idea about doing something far beyond the realm of normal life. A fantasy is something produced in the imagination, allowing you to indulge in a thought life that is very different from what you experience on a day-to-day basis. Within this realm there is no fear of discovery, no worry about being shamed; here there is only the deepest of pleasures. It is a world created in your own mind, one where you make the rules. You command the scene and choose where it goes. The possibilities are endless, but the outcome is up to you. The only limits that exist in fantasy are your own and this is the place where you can push them safely, testing yourself to find the places in your mind you may not know exists. Deep in these recesses you may find wants you never knew you had. Here, in this place, you have the freedom to luxuriate in unsated hungers.

There is safety in the world of fantasy. When a person lets go and begins to think about what they crave, a new world opens. It is one where every dream and desire can come true. There is nothing off limits in fantasy. There is nothing to be questioned about this world of indulgence.

Imagination is a safety net that catches you. There is no going too far, no need for a safe word inside your mind. This world is your creation.

Everyone has fantasies and the variations in these visions of passion vary widely. It is a natural experience that occurs in every human being. Having a rich fantasy life is not only enjoyable, but psychologically "normal." Each of us is allowed to revel in our own desires, no matter how dark or depraved they may seem; for we are the only ones that know what lies within our own imagination. Inside these erotic visions there is no shame -- only pleasure. It is a chance to dip a toe into something that may have only ever seemed a fleeting thought.

Chance encounters, the desire to watch, a visit from an unexpected stranger -- all of these things fall within a realm of normalcy. There is always a moment in stories like these, a fork in the road, when you wonder which path will be chosen. Will it end quietly, without incident, or will it move on to the next level? Here lies the difference between reality and imagination. In our minds we can proceed without hesitation to the place we might never go in our own lives. There is an opportunity to taste the forbidden and savor its sweet delights. It is only within our imaginations that we can enter into these situations with no fear and no regret.

Inside these pages are 36 tales of erotic delights that take stimulating situations and ride them to their eventual climactic end. Each one welcomes you, the reader, to enter the fantasy as an active participant, forgetting your inhibitions and taking a chance to learn what thirsts lie deep inside you.

1 THE BOSS

The whirl from the air vent built the headache that had already taken hold and I fought the urge to rub the pain away. Just my luck, I am stuck in the filing room for the afternoon with a broken air conditioner; was my luck ever going to get better? I growl as I slam shut the drawer and open another one. And why am I so agitated? Because my prick boss is making me search for files that I didn't even lose.

I can still hear his clipped voice, "Ms. Jones, the files were here and now they aren't. Since you are in charge of compiling the files for this merger, I would expect you to know where they are..."

He had stopped talking but his steel gray eyes had finished what he was saying. I was the one who had messed up and I was going to be the one to fix it. Forget that Gary from accounting was the last person to have them when he was running over numbers again; Mr. Tristen Black had left the files with me originally so it was my fault they were missing. Actually, everything that went wrong in this office was my fault according to the guy.

He was always on me about everything. My office was

too unorganized, even when it was as neat as a pin. My clothes, even the pencil skirt and tailored jacket and blouse I was wearing today, was too casual. My long, blonde hair, caught up in a tight bun, was too impractical. The man was completely infuriating and he ran the office with an iron fist. Part of me loved that he attacked business the way he attacked any lapse in my work, but part of me was ready to quit. Working for a guy that was as tightly wound as him was losing its appeal, despite the challenge he presented to me.

Slamming another drawer closed, I grind my teeth together. What the guy needed was to get laid. That would give him something to keep his attention on and maybe he would finally relax enough to let me do my job. Not that I was overly arrogant, but I was the most competent person in his office. I did my work ahead of schedule and I never backed down from a challenge...even when that challenge was Tristen Black.

And that is why I am in a dusty filing closet searching for the file that Gary believes he filed by mistake because I never backed down from a challenge. Crying out in triumph, I snatched up the missing files and marched out of the closet to Tristen's office.

"Ms. Jones...you can't..."

The sound of Tristen's secretary fades as I close the office door and take in the large man sitting at the desk. To say Tristen was wet dream material is an understatement. His wide, muscular shoulders tapered down into a trim waist that was highlighted perfectly in his tailored suit. His dark hair was cut short and swept to the side. A light dusting of stubble grazed his jaw from the late hour and gave him a feral appeal. And his eyes, the steel gray eyes would burn into you and he used them in the boardroom whenever he was negotiating the latest merger. Men felt nervous and women were ready to melt under that strong gaze.

Right now, that gaze was focused on me with a

disapproving glint but his gaze had lost its effect on me long ago. After several years of being at the beck and call and whims of this man, day and night, I was not impressed by him at all. Tossing the files onto his desk, I give him a wry grin.

"There are the files, Mr. Black. Now, if you don't need anything further, I have important work to do."

With that, I quickly turn on my heel and march out of the sleek and stylish office. I can't help but smile at the look of disbelief on Tristen's face as the door clicks shut behind me.

Slipping into my small office, I sigh in relief. The small, white desk wasn't much but it was a starting point. Decorating the walls of the small office were some photos of my family and a few plants offered a bit of green to the room. As I opened up my laptop, my private line began ringing.

"Hello, Ms. Jones' office, Samantha Jones speaking."

"Hey girl, are you still coming tonight?"

Grinning, I lean back in my black office chair and gaze out the small window. "Alicia, how are you? I think I'm coming, but I don't know if he'll let me go early."

"Is he still giving you a hard time?" Alicia's voice was full of laughter and all the tension I had felt earlier was gone. She has been my best friend since we were kids and I can never hold on to my anger when I hear her voice.

"Yeah," I sigh, a grin spreading across my face, "What I really think he needs is to get laid. I am sure a good fuck will loosen him up tons and make everyone's life better."

"Really? And are you just the girl to do it?"

I laugh, "Well, maybe. I would happily spread my legs and let him slide it in if it meant him being nicer to everyone. A fucking *please* isn't too much to ask for."

The sound of her laughter almost cuts out the sound of a throat being cleared behind me and I squeeze my eyes closed.

"Umm, Alicia, can I give you a call back?"

I hang up before she can reply and I turn my chair slowly as I open my eyes. Standing in the doorway is none other than the man I was talking about. Swallowing the embarrassment that has leapt into my throat, I say, "Can I help you with anything Mr. Black?"

His eyes twinkle but I can't tell if he is laughing silently or furious about what I said. He places a stack of papers on my desk.

"I need 10 copies of this report immediately."

Jumping out of my seat, I snatch up the papers and run past him standing in my way, I feel his heat as I brush by and heat stains my cheeks red. I feel as flustered as a schoolgirl and I sigh in relief when I reach the copy room. I am a complete idiot, I chide myself as the copier starts copying the papers. Placing my head in my hands, I shake my head. "Six years of college and grad school and this is where I am. Making dumb comments about my boss and fetching him copies for a living."

My shoulders tense at the sound of him clearing his throat again. Can today get any worse? Straightening, I say to the wall above the copier, "Mr. Black, I will have those copies to you shortly."

I don't bother to look back but I can feel him hesitate at the door. Holding my breath, I will him to leave.

"See that you do," he says, before he walks away.

I glance back at the door to find it empty before turning back to the copier. All I can do is make it through today and then take the weekend to start looking for a new job. With everything that has happened today, there is no doubt that I am this close to being fired.

With the finished report in my hands, I walk back to his office. I give an apologetic shrug to Mrs. Matthews for the way I acted earlier and say, "I am here to give Mr. Black his reports."

The light in the office is dim and Tristen is sitting in the chair behind his mahogany desk staring out the window at the impressive skyline.

"Here are the reports Mr. Black."

"Leave them on the desk."

I hesitate as I drop the reports onto the cool wood, my gaze taking in his profile and the tightness of his jaw. His voice had been strange; full of tension and not his usual no nonsense tone. I turn to leave.

"Stop," he says.

My hand freezes on the doorknob and fear lances through me. This is the first time that I felt unsure with this man. I can't see him but I hear the intercom crackle to life. "Mrs. Matthews, you can head home now. I am just finalizing the reports that Ms. Jones took forever to find this morning."

My teeth grind together at his words, anger replacing the moment of fear that I had. I turn and find him standing in front of the desk, his position cocky and assured. "And please lock up the office so I am not disturbed for the rest of the evening."

"Yes sir." Mrs. Matthews's voice fills the room before Tristen turns off the intercom.

Turning his gaze towards me, I take an involuntary step backwards at the heat in his gaze.

"We need to talk Ms. Jones...about the things you said on the phone earlier. Tell me, did you really mean it?"

I feel a shrill of excitement course over my skin and I lick my lips in anticipation. He was challenging me and now was my chance to let him know exactly how I felt. Feeling like a warrior queen, I take a step and then another towards him. My finger sticks out like a sword as I gently prod his chest, ignoring the hardness of it as I do.

"Yes, yes, I meant every word. You do need to get laid! You need to lighten up. I don't care if I lose my job – I am the best damn employee you have and I am worth more than being barked at daily and making copies!"

With that, I turn but feel his hand grab my wrist, pulling me back. Excitement flushes my cheeks and I can't help but notice the pulse in my body or the wetness that is pooling below. This is turning me on, which is not good. I gaze up at his eyes in challenge, wanting him to let me go but part of me wanting to do more. Rage against him until we are both sweaty and panting.

The silver in his eyes turns liquid as he takes me in and he stares at my lips. His one hand draws up and his thumb caresses my jaw as he murmurs, "So let's see if you are as good as you proclaim," he whispers before dragging me against him.

His kiss sears my mouth as the hard lines of his body press against me. I can feel the hard shaft against my hip and I can't help myself as I grind against it, bringing a groan from him as I do. My arms wrap around him as he deepens the kiss, his tongue plunging into my mouth, licking me as passion travels across my body. I groan and pull him down to my height as his hands slide down my ass.

He pulls my skirt up around my hips and the cool air laps at my heated flesh. Picking me up, he wraps my long legs around his waist and drops his head to my neck. Nibbling up and down my neck, I rock against him, moaning at the need that is building inside of me. He stumbles against the desk and the reports that I had carefully collated fly into the air before landing in a mess on the floor, completely ruined. He pushes me down on the cool mahogany and I groan at the mixture of sensations.

Looking down at me, the question is clear in his eyes. I nod, panting out the words, "Tristen, don't fucking stop!"

He grins at the way I say his first name and I feel the buttons of my blouse pop before they fly into the air and out of sight. He chuckles at my gasp and bites my nipple through my silk bra before he moves the fabric out of the way. His tongue cools my skin as he lavishes the nipple and then moves to the other. His thumb strokes my slit through my silk panties and I squirm under his ministrations. Pushing the fabric to the side, he caresses my clit and I buck in excitement.

"I need to get inside you Samantha," he groans, his eyes feverish. "I can't wait any longer."

"Then do it," I croak, my own need wanting me to do anything but wait any longer.

Dropping his pants around his ankles, I gasp at the size of him. It looks too big to fit in me but he doesn't give me a chance to doubt before he tears my panties off and thrusts inside me. I scream and my legs wrap around him pulling him deeper inside without even thinking about it. When he is buried to the hilt, he stops and his sweat is breaking out on his brow as he fights his orgasm. His eyes burn into me, as he waits for me to get accustomed to his size.

As my body begins to accept his girth, I nod my head and he begins to move with an aching slowness that has me throwing my head back in ecstasy. His kisses descend on my neck and tension begins to build as he pulls out to the tip and then slowly slides it back to the hilt. Again and again he moves; each thrust pushing me closer to my orgasm as his teeth rake my neck.

I slip my hands under his shirt and my nails bite into the flesh of his ass pulling him into me harder. His thrusts speed up, going deeper than I ever thought possible and I can hear our combined groans echoing through the room.

Spots of lights begin to fill my vision and as he makes one hard thrust into me, I hear him roar with his orgasm, which sends me into mine. I pulse around his thickness, milking him as wave after wave of ecstasy washes over me. The lights that had been building in my vision explode and I find myself screaming out my own orgasm.

As I start to come back to myself, I hear him chuckle. He leans in to me, places another searing kiss on my lips and with gray eyes dancing in mirth, he says, "I am going to need another ten copies. Please."

2 THE NEXT DOOR NEIGHBOR

He had moved in only a few weeks before and since then, he had become one of my guilty pleasures. I loved watching him fix up the old colonial, watching it take shape and become something beautiful. As beautiful as he was with his firm body, dark, ebony skin and shaved head. His shoulders were wide, his waist trim and his chest hard. I couldn't believe how hot he was.

I saw him every day as I finished my six mile run. Ever since my divorce three years earlier, I had run and lifted weights three times a week. I was in peak shape and looked great, but I never got more than a wave from him.

He was there today as I was finishing up my run, the sweat running down my skin, my long red hair stuck to my scalp, ponytail hanging limply. My small breasts were held with a tight, bra tank top and my running shorts were tight and short. I could see him hammering away on the veranda and I slowed to a walk to cool down.

I could picture him putting down his hammer and slowly walking over to me. He would gather me up into his arms and carry me back to his house where he would make love to me for hours. I could imagine how big his cock was as it slid into me.

Shaking myself from my thoughts, I dared a glance his way. Today, he wasn't lifting his hands in greeting. Instead, he seemed completely oblivious to me. Shaking the disappointment I felt, I began running again, but as I neared his house, I saw him raise his hand and wave. I waved back and instead of heading on, I took a deep breath and headed in his direction.

I couldn't take my eyes off of his wide chest, sweat beading on his ebony skin, and I was grateful that I was wearing my shades or he would be able to see exactly where I was looking. As I crossed his driveway, my feet tangled in a cord and I crashed to the ground. Embarrassment flooded my pale cheeks with pink and I noticed the shop vac I had tripped over. Really, I tripped on something that freaking big? I groaned inwardly.

When I glanced up, a grin spread across my lips as I saw him laughing as he raced to my side. I sat up on the ground and started laughing as I covered my face with my hands. I felt him kneel down beside me and his large hands slid over my leg as he checked my ankle.

"Are you okay?" His voice was deep and ran over my skin, raising goose bumps on my flesh.

"Yes," I managed. "Nothing like perfect first impressions." I glanced up at him and nearly melted under his chocolate brown gaze.

"You're name wouldn't happen to be Grace, would it?" I nodded. "Well, I'm Stan. Do you want to come in for a cold drink?"

I shook my head, trying to find my voice, "Oh, I don't want to put you out."

His grin was large and infectious as he said, "It is the least I can do after causing your fall."

I grinned back and nodded, following him into the house and stylish kitchen – obviously, the big modern kitchen was the first thing he had remodeled in the house. It was breathtaking.

"You know, I have been here nearly a month and you

are the only neighbor not to introduce yourself or welcome me to the neighborhood." He said as he pulled some ice water from the fridge. He cut a lemon and placed it in the glass.

"I'm sorry. I tend to keep to myself," I said quietly, taking the glass from him.

"I see you running every day. I've often thought about joining you."

I nodded but my attention was on the woodwork of the cabinets. The intricate work was absolutely gorgeous and my hands run over the dark wood.

"You should one day. Did you make these?" I asked, but I knew the answer already.

"Yes, I have done various wood working for nearly ten years. I love it." He beamed with pride. "You know, you are the only one that has been interested in what I do or what I'm building, the rest only wanted to ask questions for gossip."

"Oh, really?" I continued to wander around the kitchen, taking in all the detail that he had put into it, "What type of gossip did they want to know?"

He stood up and walked up behind me, "Like if I am seeing anyone."

His heat flooded my senses and I longed to lean against him. "Are you?" I whispered, shivering.

"No, but there has been this beautiful red head that I have wanted to get to know for a while. I have been watching her all week and she has left me yearning to touch her silky skin."

Feathered nerves shot down my body and his words were no more than a breath on my ear. I felt his hands grasp my arms and lightning pulsed from his touch as he turned me in his arms. He placed the glass on the counter and stared down into my green eyes.

"You are the most beautiful woman I have ever seen."

Closing my eyes, I licked my lips in anticipation. It had been so long since someone told me I was beautiful. It startled me to feel his lips touch my mouth lightly and then I arched my back, tipping my head back to give him better access to me. He takes the invitation and deepens the kiss. His hands rake over my body, raising the hairs on my arms as he sent desire shooting through me.

I dug my hands into his bare back and pressed him into me. I melted into him and then the urgency of my desire burned deeper and I couldn't stop myself as I clawed at his chest and back. He growled out his passion and scooped me into his arms. I feel tiny against him and I feel a moment of panic, wondering if he was too big for me.

He moved through the house to his bedroom and tossed me onto a massive bed. I could hardly take in the craftsmanship or the colors of his room before he was kissing me again. Once on me, his hands fumbled with my top. I pressed him back and freed my breasts from the confining tank top. I slipped my shorts and panties off and reach for his jeans but he is already shedding them.

I playfully crawled backwards on the bed as he chased me, his huge cock jutting out towards me, fully erect. He pushed me back and attacked my breasts. I gasped at the need that was building at the apex of my thighs as his tongue laved at my nipple. He sucked my breast into his mouth and his hand slid down to my clit. He rubbed it until I began panting, new sweat breaking out on my skin.

I spread my legs for him and begged, "Please...take me now."

He grinned and positioned himself between my legs. His cock slid up and down my slit and I wiggled against him as my climax built. I hadn't felt this type of wanting in years and the tension sent me closer to the edge. I knew I would start coming the moment he entered me.

I ran my hands up and down his back, urging him forward. Biting down my frustration, I grabbed his ass and pulled him into me. His cock speared into me and I paused, panting at his size as my tightness adjusted to his thickness. When it did, I pulled him in the rest of the way inside and we both groan into each other's mouth.

I slid my tongue into his mouth and grasped his biceps as he pulled out almost to the tip. He thrusts back inside and I cry out at the pleasure ripping through me. I never felt so full in my life. I was swept up into passion as he continued to slam his cock into me.

His thrusts sped up and his hand moved between us, rubbing my clit with increasing urgency. My orgasm builds and I could barely breathe from the tension building in me. Then it snaps and I screamed in ecstasy. He groaned as my body began to spasm around his cock. One last thrust and he emptied himself inside me. My muscles clenched and tightened, milking every last drop out of him.

I didn't have time to relax in the aftermath before we heard loud pounding on the door.

"Who the hell is that?" Stan barked. He grabbed a sheet to wrap around his waist and headed to the door. As soon as he cleared the room I jumped up and put my clothes back on. I reached the juncture of the hallway and living room when I heard Laren, the lady from two houses down and stopped. The nerve of her! She was married, but clearly offering to come inside and straight to his bed! She kept flirting with him and ignoring his excuses as to why he needed to get back to what he was doing. Knowing she wasn't going to let him return, I walked up behind him and put my arms around his waist and kissed his back. I circled around him and looked at Laren.

"Oh, hi Laren!" I started to walk past her, but Stan caught my wrist. I turned around and stood on my tip toes. Licking his ear, I said, "Welcome to the neighborhood." Then I smiled at Laren and continued walking, heading to my house. I had barely made it to the end of the porch when I heard his throaty laugh.

"This is isn't over." He yelled at me, and shut the door in Laren's face.

3 THE EX

I could sense him staring at me and I wondered if he realized who I was or if he was simply enjoying my trim legs beneath my skirt. I wasn't sure, but I bet he didn't know who I was. I wasn't upset about it. I haven't seen my ex-boyfriend, Logan, in ten years. The last time was when we were in college and we broke up. We were different people then. I was the shy college girl battling the college thirty, bad hair and bad skin. I was timid and he was outgoing. How we even hooked up in the first place was a mystery.

We ended the relationship mutually after about a month. He was going to Europe with his family and I was going to graduate school. We promised to stay in touch but promises were broken. I went on to graduate. I lost my shy demeanor along with the bad hair, bad skin, and thirty pounds. He had gone on to run his parents' company; the very company I was negotiating a merger with.

As my boss introduces me to the room, I see his eyes light up. There is no doubt that he remembers me now. I try to ignore the way he is staring at me throughout the meeting – he is looking at me like he is undressing me, trying to find the girl I used to be. I manage to make it through the meeting somehow. The numbers and reasons why the merger is beneficial are flying out of my head as I race towards the door before he can capture me.

But I'm too late and I feel his hand close over my wrist. "Selene," he sighs my name and I feel old desire awaken inside me. "It has been so long. How have you been?"

I stare up into his dark green eyes and feel like the little girl he used to know – timid and shy. Swallowing the feeling down, I toss my dark hair over my shoulder and say, "I've been good. Very busy as you can see, but I'm doing well. How about you?"

His eyes narrow at the challenge in my voice and he says, "Why don't we meet for dinner tonight so we can catch up?" I glance around at the nearly empty room, looking for an excuse to decline. "I also have more questions about the merger," he adds quickly.

Sighing, I nod. "Okay, I will meet you in the lobby of your hotel at about seven."

With that, I head out the door to the safety of my office, chiding myself the entire way about my weakness around this man.

****

The lobby is empty when I reach the hotel and I sigh. It's just like Logan to have something planned. Reaching the desk, I say, "Could you ring up to Mr. Logan Gardel and let him know that Selene Buchannan is here?"

"Ms. Buchannan? Mr. Gardel is expecting you on the rooftop." The desk clerk hands me a key card. "Just take the elevator to the top floor and insert the card to gain access to the rooftop garden."

I roll my eyes and take the card in hand. "And it's just like Logan to pull out all the stops," I mumble under my breath.

As I step out onto the rooftop garden, my breath

catches. It is amazing. The air is heavy with the smell of night blooming flowers and a thousand twinkle lights sparkle in the darkness. Surrounding the hotel are the lights of the city, but the sound of the streets are faded. In the center of all this beauty is a table set for two with candlelight and wine cooling beside it. Logan is standing beside the table, looking out across the city and I suddenly feel frumpy in the simple dress I chose to wear with him looking casual, but elegant in his khakis and grey polo shirt.

"Selene," he smiles as he gestures to the table and pulls my seat out for me.

I return the smile as I slide into the chair, but I can feel the tension in my shoulders. As much as I have grown, I can still feel the girl who had been completely enamored by him pushing to escape from my body.

"You look amazing," he says as he pours the wine. "You have such a different body now...not that I didn't like you before but you definitely look amazing."

A blush floods my cheeks and I take a sip of my wine to hide my reaction to him. I look up at him and his eyes rake over my body. I can't help the thrill of excitement that courses through me. I take in his physique, perfectly shown through the tight shirt. He has definitely been hitting the gym himself.

"You look great too," I say on a wispy breath.

"I hope you don't mind, but I arranged the meal," he says slipping into his seat and motioning to the waiter I just noticed.

I blush even deeper at the thoughts that had been running through my head. If I had listened to them, I would have been screwing him on the table in front of that waiter right now.

As the first dish is placed in front of me, the friendly conversation flows as easily as wine. I am amazed at how natural it feels to be sitting across from him, both of us giving all the details of our lives between when we broke up until this very moment. It is easy, but what isn't easy is the electricity that is crackling in the air between us.

I feel it in every glance, the way that he keeps staring at me like he wants to devour me and not the food. I feel naked in front of him, but I don't mind. Every time his hand brushes against me, I feel an awakening. My body has been waiting so long to feel this man's touch again that I am practically humming when the chocolate dessert is served. I grin wickedly, "Chocolate mousse with sprinkles and whipped cream...you remembered."

His smile is wicked. "How could I forget after that night when you covered me in it." Turning to the waiter, he says, "That's all for the now. You can leave and I will call you when we need everything cleared."

And with those words, we are alone to enjoy our dessert. I take a bite of it and moan in pleasure. It is the best mousse I have ever tasted.

"Do you have to eat it like that?" He groans and I look over to see him rubbing the bulge in his pants.

I lick the spoon, making a slight purr while I do before licking the chocolate off of my lips. I don't answer him or even acknowledge what I am doing to him. If he wants me, he can work for it.

"You are making me so hot watching you eat that dessert," he groans and stands up.

Anticipation fills me as he stares down at me and I want him to take me right there, but as he turns to walk away, I can't help the disappointment I feel. He walks to a wall and presses a button. The soft sounds of my favorite band fill the air and set a seductive mood in the garden.

Walking back to me, he extends his large hand and says, "Dance with me."

I nod, feeling hypnotized by Logan as he slips his arms around me. They burn where he touches me and his entire body sears me as he pulls me close. I can't help but notice the hard bulge digging into my hip as I press against it, moaning.

He buries his face into my hair and I can feel him inhaling my scent. His own smell smothers me and it feels familiar and exciting at the same time. My hands run up and down his strong arms before they slip around his neck. He places a small kiss on my ear and I shudder in response but he doesn't do more. Instead, his fingers slip down the sides of my body as though he is remembering my shape – learning how well the new me fits against him.

The soft cotton of my dress does nothing to hide the effect he is having on me. My nipples are hard pebbles poking through my sun dress and I capture his hands sliding down my body. He stops, his eyes questioning, wondering if I am the same shy girl I used to be. They widen in surprise as I move his hands to my breasts and gasp at the tension already building in me.

He takes my direction and his thumbs begin to circle the nipple as his hands cup my breasts. I pull his head towards me and press kisses to his lips. Teasing at first and then with more urgency as his fingers continue to work my nipples sending tremor after tremor through me. I can feel the heat building between my legs and I know it won't take long before I am crying out his name.

As we kiss, he takes control and his tongue invades my body. He lifts me up and I wind my legs around his waist as we dance. His groin rubs slowly against my slit and I can feel the burning tension growing in my body. I begin to pant as his fingers dig into my ass and I am so thankful that I wore a thong today.

He growls in excitement and places me on the side of the table. I hear, rather than see, the dishes crashing to the floor and then I am laying on my back across the table, my legs opened wide as he stares down at me like I am the feast that he is waiting for.

Squeezing my nipple through my dress, I cry out at the need I am feeling, "Please, take me Logan!" I groan but he shakes his head and continues to suck and knead my nipples through my dress. I try to pull him up so he can thrust his cock into me, but he pushes my hands away and slides down the table.

Placing my legs on his shoulder, he thumbs the thin piece of fabric of my panties to the side, his fingers teasing my slit before he plunges his tongue deep inside of me. My hips jerk at the eroticism and I can picture how I look, spread out on the table, my head thrashing back and forth from the pleasure his tongue is spreading across my body.

He licks my clit before sucking it into his mouth and the stars above me fill my vision. My head whirls at the passion filling me to the brim and before I realize it, I am screaming out my orgasm as he laps up the liquid spilling from me.

Without giving me time to catch my breath, he slides his cock inside me, driving all the way in and groaning. I gasp as a second orgasm builds deep in my core as he thrusts hard and fast – almost like he is making up for those ten years we lost.

I am swept up in the current as I buck against him, screaming his name. His hips rock wildly against mine as his thrusts get even harder and faster. I can hear him cry out his orgasm as he says my name over and over again.

Finished, he collapses against my quivering body and says, "I'll never let you get away from me again."

4 THE WAITRESS

I walk into the restaurant carrying my large laptop bag feeling stressed and a bit weary. I need a drink. I was told by corporate that I need to update the proposal I had worked on for two months and wasn't even sure where to start. All I know is that I need sustenance and a quiet, friendly atmosphere to calm me while I send the required emails to the big wigs of Ash and Wilson. I need relaxation before I head home to hours of even more work.

I step up to the hostess stand and ask for my regular booth, if it was available. She nods and leads me back to the curtain-covered area which seems like a private sanctuary to me. I've hosted corporate dinners in this very booth and knew that I wouldn't be disturbed by the public. All I had to do was push the curtains closed and I was alone, aside from Katie.

Katie was the main reason I frequented the Turine. She was not only an efficient and productive waitress, one that never missed a beat when it came to orders or drink refills, but she was also exquisitely beautiful. Her long dark hair was usually braided down her back, which only served to highlight her straight nose and big blue eyes that seemed to torch me like a laser each time she looked at me. Tuesdays were her days off, so I was disappointed that I wouldn't see her tonight.

I take out my laptop and open it on the table, plug in the necessary wires as I decide on what drink I need after this horrible day of frustration. With the computer powered on, I type in my email password and commence writing to my superior my plans for the re-draft.

I was caught up in my message and startled by her cheerful voice, "Hey, Jason. How are you? Can I get you a drink? By the look on your face I can tell you need something strong. Is this a beer or scotch kind of day?" It was her. Oh boy. Katie's tight-fitting button-up white blouse set off her bronzed skin and somehow magnified her large, perky breasts. I clear my throat and try not to stare at her full mouth.

"Hi Katie. I need a scotch, neat. It's been one of those days."

She smiles and murmurs, "Sure thing," and heads toward the bar. I watch her ass as it sways underneath the short black skirt as she walks away. My groin grows tight as I imagine her nude; full breasts, tight ass, and legs that never stop.

I turn my attention back to the email, trying to focus. Katie's face clouds my mind as I try to explain my need for more expenditure from the construction department. I'm typing my last sentence when Katie's face appears again. She smiles and hands me a glass of the restaurant's best scotch. Our fingers graze one another as I take the glass. I set the drink on a coaster while she proceeds to tell me about the night's specials.

"Filet mignon with garlic and Thai butter sauce, grilled salmon with roasted squash and potatoes, and a nice quail and polenta dish." I stare at her for a few seconds before I register that she was giving me a rundown of the evening's chef specials. "Would you like to order now or wait a bit until you finish your work?" she asks.

"Whatever you think," I mutter as I mentally slap

myself back into reality. I really need to stop imagining her long legs wrapped around my back. I flirt with her, and I ask her if she wants to join my party of one. As always, she playfully slaps my shoulder and rolls her eyes.

"Jason, I swear you'll get me fired one day. You know I can't do that." As always, she turns down my half-hearted flirtations and saunters away with a backwards glance that could bring a million men to their knees.

I turn my attention back to the computer screen and begin a new email to Bob Billings, the CEO of the company. This is going to be a tough one, knowing my job was on the line if I don't perform to his standards. While I type, I glance up to see Katie looking at me between her long black lashes from the bar. More than once I notice this, assuming she was waiting for me to finish my drink. I took a giant gulp of my scotch and put my head back down to my task at hand.

I'm so involved in my work that I hardly notice when Katie arrives at my table, a fresh scotch in her hand.

"It's been one hell of a long day, I can tell. This one's on me." I notice my empty drink and try to remember drinking it all. "I'm here if you need anything else", she happily says while looking into my tired eyes. I'm still focused on the computer screen when I say, "I need you in my bed." Katie slowly turns and walks away, mumbling something under her breath. Damn, I was focusing too hard on my work - I can't believe I just said that out loud.

I bend my head down to continue the arduous task of placating my bosses while simultaneously taking sips of the smooth scotch that Katie had brought to me. The liquor was finally settling in and the day starts melting away as I continue to work.

I'm taken aback when Katie suddenly appears, shutting the velvet curtains behind her. She stares at me with her deep dark eyes and states hesitantly, "I only have fifteen minutes. This isn't your bed but it will have to do." She pushes the table back and steps away from the computer cord; a look of apprehension on her lovely face.

She stands in front of me, unbuttons her starched white blouse from the top and slowly makes her way down to the bottom buttons. She pulls her shirt wide to display her enormous breasts that seem to be spilling out of the cups of her lacy white bra. I see her nipples harden underneath the thin fabric. She leans toward my face, searching my eyes, before giving me a soft kiss on the lips. My cock responds with movement at just the slightest touch of her mouth upon mine. She notices that I accept her sweet advances and steps closer, allowing me to pull her nipples into my mouth over the soft fabric of her bra. Katie reaches up and pulls down the lacy cups, revealing large hard nipples, standing straight out and begging for more attention. I immediately bury my face between them, feeling the warmth as she moans. I attack one nipple, then the other, nipping at them with my teeth. She throws her head back with the force of a wild stallion as I suck on one nipple while reaching my hand up under that sexy black skirt, tracing the lines of her ass and slipping my fingers under her underwear.

I need this so badly. My body aches for this woman. I pull down her panties ever so slowly; my fingers savor the feel of her long legs. Her breathing becomes heavier as I find her soft and very wet center. She inhales sharply as I insert a finger deep inside of her. She hurriedly unbuckles the belt on my pants to free my hardness, allowing it to stand straight and tall. My finger still inside her, she says in a breathy voice, "Time is running out."

Katie straddles me, impaling herself onto to my throbbing cock. Her silken wetness envelopes the length of my shaft and I am in heaven. I watch her face as she rides me up and down so fast that I become intoxicated. It isn't the scotch, it is Katie. Her deep pounding lights a fuse inside me that I cannot control. It feels like a well of yearning inside of me is about to explode.

She groans as we meet each other's thrusts. Her wetness is sliding up and down my cock so fast that I can barely remember where I am. I grab her hips and I come hard, so hard that stars fill my eyesight, I moan loudly and Katie throws her hand over my mouth. Katie slows down and quits moving trying to catch her breath. I can feel her orgasm draining every last drop from my quivering balls. Her eyes are dark and full of lust as she meets my gaze while leaning towards me.

"Are you ready to order now? I hear the filet is fantastic." She says as she slowly eases herself up, squeezing me as she goes, and pulls on her panties.

"I'll have the filet then." I say already feeling the void from her absence, "And afterwards, I'll have you again…for dessert."

5 THE POOL MAN

The sun shines down on the pool and I sigh at the small amount of dirt that is in the water. I was hoping the pool guy would have been out before I got up so I could spend the day hanging out by the pool with a few of my friends. We were looking forward to a girl's day with drinks, some sun, and swimming. As I shake my head, the phone rings.

"Hello?"

"Ms. Jacobs?" the man on the other end said.

"Yes."

"This is Oasis Pools; I was just phoning to let you know that your regular pool guy called in sick so we will be sending a replacement for you. We wanted to let you know so you weren't surprised when he came to the house."

"Okay, thanks for letting me know."

I sighed inwardly. This was the worst luck. Now we would be in the middle of our girl's day and we would have that fat pool guy show up.

Within an hour, my friends were gathered in the kitchen and we were already drinking wine. I was laughing at a particularly dirty joke when the doorbell rang. I answered the door and my mouth dropped open. My regular, old pool man was gone and in his place was a Spartan god. He looked like he had just descended Olympus with his dark brown hair and blue eyes. His chiseled good looks and athletic build made me instantly wet.

"Ms. Jacobs, I'm Nate. I'm here to service your pool." His voice was deep and I felt it right at the apex of my thighs.

I nodded and invited him in. Taking him through the house, I could feel his eyes on my bikini clad ass and I couldn't help but smile with pride. I had a nice body; I knew it and I worked to keep it looking that way. I took him into the kitchen, where my friends stared at him with the same desire I was sure was in my eyes.

"Ladies, this is Nate, the pool guy. He's going to get it ready for us."

I took him out to the pool and showed him where the equipment was. Then I returned to the girls in the kitchen but we watched him through the window as he took off his shirt and began cleaning out the pool. We drank our wine and drooled over the new pool boy. We sounded like children as we sighed and giggled with everything that he did. My mouth watered and I felt hot for him.

As he was finishing up, the girls started leaving to head home. I showed them to the door and then went back to the pool area.

"Do you mind servicing the hot tub as well? It really needs it."

He smiled and cleared his throat. "Sure."

I pointed to the hot tub room and then went back to the house. I lay down on the couch and ran my fingers over my bare skin where my bikini was not covering it. I slid my hands into the bikini bottoms and thought about how his chest had shimmered with his sweat as he worked. I thought of the way his flat chiseled stomach moved and the way his sculpted ass flexed each time he bent over. My fingers rubbed my clit and I groaned as I brought myself closer to a satisfying, albeit solo, climax. I spread my legs giving myself better access to my center. Shutting my eyes, I bit my lip as my orgasm was almost there. I could almost feel his shaft filling me as I fixated on his image in my mind, and then the knock at the door pulled me from my dream.

I pulled my hand from my bottoms and walked down the hallway to the back door. Opening it, I realized that I had forgotten my wrap. His eyes widened at the sight of my flushed body in my bikini and I fought the urge to pull him against me and scratch the itch that I had created between my legs.

He cleared his throat. "Umm, the door is locked to the hot tub room. Can I get the key?"

I nodded and raced back to the kitchen. Rummaging in the drawer, I pulled out the key and headed back to the door. I led him outside to the hot tub room and unlocked the door. Walking inside, I showed him the motor and the various equipment that needed to be serviced. He reached down to grab a tag that hung off the door to the motor and then looked at me confused - the equipment showed to be serviced last week.

I turned around to face him and his gaze burned into my body. I shuddered at the pure desire running through his eyes. I pause in what I am saying and I swallow deeply. He had stopped me before I satisfied myself and I still needed more. I don't know if it was because I had gone a year without sex or if it was simply all the wine I had, but I swallowed my inhibitions.

Walking up to him, I wrapped my arms around him and planted a kiss on his jaw line. I inched up his face, kissing and biting his skin until I reached his full lips.

I swept my tongue deep inside his mouth, kissing him passionately before I pulled away slightly. He gazed down at me for a brief second and I waited for him to push me away. Instead, he pulled me in tighter, my breasts pressed flat against his chest, and he captured my mouth in his. My clit throbbed with need and fire flowed through me, awakening passion I hadn't felt in a long time.

His tongue slid into my mouth and I sucked on it. I moaned as his hands cupped my breasts. One hand drifted around to untie my bikini top and he pulled it away, exposing my bare breasts to him. The rough pads of his fingers grazed my nipples, bringing them to hard peaks. He grasped both nipples between thumb and forefinger and I groaned as he pinched and sent sensations down my belly.

I bit into his neck, panting with need for him to fill me. He slid his hands down my body, awakening my skin and the coil of heat inside me. He pushed my bottoms off and his fingers parted the folds of my slit. His feverish kiss turned into a smile against my swollen mouth as he felt the wetness pouring from me. As he slid a finger deep inside me I began to rock against his hand.

My hands roamed over his body as his finger continued to fuck me and I could barely stand as my orgasm came closer. I pushed his shorts down and he kicked his legs free.

Bracing me against the wall, he lifted me up by grabbing my ass and then he positioned his engorged head at the entrance of my tightness. I groaned loudly as he pressed his solid length deep into my slick depths, slamming me against the wall.

He thrusted up and down and I began to ride his cock. I clenched around it as my orgasm shattered through me. I bit into his neck again and it sent him over the edge. He grunted, growling as he comes, his hot seed filling me to overflowing.

"That was amazing," I whispered into his neck, still drunk with the desire coursing through my sated body.

We both laughed as he held me against the wall and I felt completely satisfied. As I melted against him, he leaned down with a twinkle in his eyes, "The hot tub was serviced last week…but I guess you already knew that." I flashed a mischievous smile and he kissed me again, giving promise of another good service.

6 THE TEACHER

I was late for my first French tutelage and was nervous. I rushed into the well-lit classroom expecting to be yelled at by an old man with an iron fist. Instead, I saw what seemed to be a goddess sitting behind a desk, who lifted her blonde head up from a large stack of papers and said, "Oh, how nice of you to join me Monsieur Mason. Let's begin as I'm busy and it's been a long day." I swallowed nervously as I was the only student. I really didn't need any more pressure. Being late was one thing, being the only student was another.

Madame Dusant stood up from her desk and I couldn't help but notice her body. I looked from her breasts down to her shapely legs. Her suit, although professional, showed off the curve of her breasts and she wore black heels that accentuated the shape of her calves perfectly. Of course, she noticed my gaze wandering over her body and I quickly bent my head and stared at my open notebook instead. She made her way to the front of the board and I looked up at her. Her blonde hair was in a loose bun and her black-framed glasses were slipping down her nose.

She smiled softly and said, "Now that you are finally

here, let's get down to business." Her French accent didn't go unnoticed as the bulge in my pants began to swell.

I was told to open my college French book, which I had forgotten to take out of my bag. I quickly unzipped my backpack and laid the book on the table, turning to page 22 as instructed. I glanced up as Madame was writing basic French verbs on the board, but I couldn't take my eyes off of her breasts. She wore a silk shirt under her suit jacket and the edges of her breasts were peeking out at me, almost daring me to lick them.

She was writing French terms so fast on the board that my mind couldn't keep up. Madame wore fine French fishnet stockings and I knew that there was a garter belt holding them up over her sumptuous thighs. I forced myself to concentrate on the terms that now covered the blackboard and when she told me to focus, my mind only focused on one thing; Madame's luscious figure. She walked towards my desk and leaned over to look at my work.

"Merdi," she whispered under her breath as she walked to the front of the classroom and begin explaining again how important accents were in the French language.

My face was flushed as she proceeded to slap her yard-stick at the board in front of every French verb there was, raising her voice yet trying to sound polite as she told me to pronounce the foreign words in front of me. I tried, I really did try. The scent of her exotic perfume wafted towards me as she paced; the notes of wisteria and lilac filled my senses as I tried to understand why French verbs were backwards in sentences. The only thing in French that I understood was how she moved, spoke, and made my pulse race.

I became frustrated by the ambience her entire being created and trying to learn something that I could not concentrate on. Madame looked at me for a moment and slowly put her stick down. She walked forward and closed my book that lay on the desk in front of me after I had buried my head in my hands, ready to give up.

"Cherie, it is okay." She sat at the desk in front of me and lifted my head out of my hands. Her straightforward gaze led me to hold hers with my own.

Her green eyes stared into mine as she explained that it was okay. We had many more sessions ahead and that she knew it was frustrating. She gave one last look at my forlorn face and sighed. She went to her desk and quickly wrote something on a notepad. She walked back to me, her high heels clicking on the floor.

"Here, call me when you need to. You study. This day has been hectic and I need to get off my feet." I took the paper from her perfectly manicured hand and tucked it into my notebook. She leaned over my desk and with a twinkle in her eye stated, "Anytime you need to, mon chere, call me." I blushed as she licked her bottom lip and stood.

"Anytime?" I stuttered to her.

"Oui, anytime," she answered. I was so deeply embarrassed for staring at her graceful body and focusing on the French accent that rolled off her tongue that I didn't realize she had walked behind me. She massaged my shoulders, relaxing the nervous tension that had been shooting through my body. I leaned into it and let her fingers push into my neck muscles. Whatever she was doing with her adept fingers felt amazing and as soon as I was feeling relaxed, she stopped suddenly and walked towards her desk.

I hurriedly gathered my things. I was a mess, yet I wanted her so badly. My cock was getting harder by the second as I walked towards the book case in the front of the classroom, pretending to scan the titles. Her eyes had said she wanted me and I decided to take a chance. I glanced over at her desk and noticed that she was sitting in her chair, pulling her shoes off and unpinning her long blonde hair. I dialed her number and waited for her to answer.

She looked over at me and smiled as she answered the call. My heart started racing again as I watched her stand up from her chair, murmuring something in French. Her voice was as seductive as her body was as she walked towards me, throwing off her suit jacket and unbuttoning her blouse. She kept speaking words foreign to me as she unleashed her enhanced breasts from the black bra she wore. They seemed to bounce as she got closer.

My cock became rock hard as she stood in front of me. I immediately attacked her nipples, going for one and then the other as she moaned, "Oui, cherie, oui!" I flicked them quickly with my tongue as she held the back of my head. I reached around and grabbed her firm ass, and went to her full lips, licking and kissing the sweet softness.

She pulled away and asked me something in French. I stared into her mesmerizing eyes and mumbled, "Vous oui?" She slapped me, hard, on the cheek and proceeded to ask me another question.

"Garcon fromage," I whispered and she then slapped me again on the other cheek.

"Non!" she violently said as I was trailing my fingers up her slender back. She slapped me again, causing my face to sting in pain.

All of my fears seemed to vanish as I ravaged her body with my hands and tongue until her moaning stopped. She grabbed my shirt collar and pushed me onto the floor of the classroom. I wasn't sure what Madame would do next but before my thoughts became my worst fears, she reached down and skillfully undid my pants. I helped her pull them down as she reached to pull up her skirt. All I could mutter was "Oui, Madame" as I saw that she wore no panties with her garter belt and stockings. I didn't think I could contain my lust as she slid down on my cock, slowly, but expertly and all the way to the bottom.

I felt like a French prince as she rode my swollen hardness up and down. I tried not to come; she was clearly enjoying this tryst. Madame reached down with her fingers to find her clit, rubbing it until I felt her begin to get even wetter than before. Her other hand went to her hard nipples, pinching and playing with them. She grunted passionately as I grabbed her hips, grinding her center onto my cock, never missing a beat. The tempo of our thrusting hips became more frantic as I felt her tighten inside, a glorious feeling which made me release all that I had deep inside her pulsing wetness. She shuddered and wiped the small beads of sweat off of her delicate upper lip.

Silently, she grabbed my hand and put one of my fingers in her mouth and sucked extremely hard. My cock jumped back to attention. She stared down at me and whispered in her seductive accent, "Are you ready for lesson two?"

7 THE SOCCER MOM

Today was the day. It was the soccer party of the season and Sharon was hosting it this year. Our sons had played together on the same team for three seasons and all the kids were excited, yet not as excited as I was to see Sharon. Her smiling face and charming personality had quelled the boredom of more than one soccer game during seasons that seemed to stretch on forever.

I made sure Brendan gathered the Buffalo wings and dip, while I grabbed the hostess gift, a bottle of wine. I had a feeling she would need it after today. Sharon had been single for years, and her generosity never wavered. She always had a smile on her a face and a kind word for every person she met. Although she knew I had been divorced for five years, she never seemed to have shown anything except a casual interest in me.

I hurried Brendan to the car. I had promised Sharon that I would arrive early to inflate the bouncy house that was to be set up in her back yard. I didn't want to disappoint the children or Sharon. We settled ourselves into the car and drove towards Sharon's house, Brendan talking all the way there about who would be at the party and what fun activities Sharon had planned. We were both excited.

Sharon had greeted us warmly and had busied herself in the kitchen after directing me to the back yard and Brendan upstairs to play video games with her son Cody. I walked outside and started blowing up the bouncy house, all the while thinking of how bright her smile was and how lovely her hair was loose, flowing over her shoulders.

There were already three other parents at the party, and I wanted this chance to talk to her on a more personal basis. I tried to ignore my thoughts and focus on the task at hand. I heard Sharon's enchanting laughter ringing out of the window and felt myself getting hard. I started imagining her breasts bare and myself inside of her. I kept working and when I was done, went in search of her for a glass of water.

I found her in the kitchen, as it seemed to be her designated area today. She had changed clothes for the party and she looked so beautiful that it was hard for me to speak. Her white tee was tight and the air-conditioning in the house highlighted her nipples, causing them to stand out against her shirt. I diverted my attention and asked for a glass of water. She filled a glass with ice water and handed it to me laughing.

"What's so funny?" I asked. She walked back to the sink and wrung out a towel; returning to me saying, "You look like you've been playing in the dirt." She wiped the grime from my forehead and down around my face. I took in the coolness of her touch. She mentioned the soccer season as she wiped my neck and we discussed scores and stats. It was small talk, but so much more.

A large group of children with their bustling parents burst into the room, causing her to drop the towel. She recovered and proceeded to hand out party favors to all of the children, looking each of them in the face and letting them know how much she loved them and was glad they were able to be at the party. The gleam in her eyes was obvious. She was more than amazing; she was a goddess who needed to be worshipped by more than her child's soccer team. I was begging inside to just help her do one more chore.

I recovered enough to join the party. Brendan and Cody were both chasing the other children in the back yard, water guns blazing. Tiring of the bouncy house, the kids had filled their guns up from the hose outside and were firing shots at one another. The parents seemed to be talking amongst themselves while watching the kids and snacking on the array of food that Sharon had laid out on the table. I didn't care about food and turned to the overflowing trashcan. I grabbed up the bag and carried it to her container in the garage, trying to help any way that I could. Entering the yard again, I watched Sharon race around with kids, laughing and finally falling down, the kids shooting her with all the ammunition they had. It was a wonderful moment for the children, but I wasn't so sure about Sharon. I could see that her white shirt was soaked and her nipples were hard and bare.

I raced towards her, grabbed my own water gun, and sprayed the kids, corralling them back to the bouncy house. I didn't want her to risk embarrassment. I talked to parents as I shielded her from any unusual gazes that may have come her way. Laughing, we made it to the house and she turned to face me, her breasts covered in a very wet shirt. She looked exquisite.

"I should probably go change. What do you think?"

"I think you look great just like this, but some of the other moms might not agree." I said, teasing.

Sharon laughed and went to the window and yelled out, "Kate, can you hold the fort down while I change?" She turned to me and smiled.

As she walked towards her bedroom all I could do was stare at her ass. She turned and nodded towards the room and kept walking. What was I to do? What did that mean?

I took her lead but not before checking outside, making sure Kate had the party under control and the kids were safe and having fun. I turned back towards the bedroom…and walked that way.

I hesitantly knocked on the bedroom door and peeked in, and then entered because what awaited me was glorious. Sharon was standing beside her bed nude. Her large breasts were pert with hard nipples. I longed to suck them. My eyes traveled down her body, from her breasts to her most private of areas; it was shaven except for a small patch of hair that seemed to beg for me to touch it. I was hard instantly.

I walked towards her after locking the door; her sly smile a new one that I had not encountered. I approached and shyly, she turned her back to me. I wiped the hair away from her neck and kissed it, taking in the warm scent of her delicate perfume. She gasped as I reached around and found her breast, embracing the full feel of it. I used my other hand to reach around to run my fingers up the inner part of her thigh, running my finger up and lingering in the patch of hair before dipping my finger in and lightly touching her clit. Sharon let out a soft moan as continued to graze my fingertips up and down her beautiful body.

Sharon turned around and looked at me. She reached up and started unbuttoning my pants. I helped her finish taking off my clothes, patiently looking at her, taking in her beautifully soft body, knowing what I was about to do. I leaned down to kiss her softly, then the harder as our growing desire reached full bloom. I leaned down and took a nipple into my mouth.

She ran her hands through my hair and whispered, "I've wanted you forever."

I looked up at her with surprise and she smiled sweetly. I grabbed her face gently between my hands. "And I have wanted you for longer."

I turned her around towards the bed and reached around to play with her clit. She cried out and bent over on her stomach. She groaned only slightly as I entered her and I took my time, slowly entering her wet folds.

"Don't go slow. I need you to fuck me hard. I need you to make me forget about everything," she pleaded. I couldn't contain my relief. I raked my fingers down her back and pulled her hair. She moaned louder as I increased the tempo. I grabbed her hips and drove hard and deep, giving her exactly what she wanted. I couldn't get enough of her firm body as I watched it move over the quaintly flowered bedspread.

She was so wet that I had to pull out so that I wouldn't explode. I pushed two fingers deep inside of her and leaned down to kiss her neck.

"I've wanted you for so long. I need you inside me. Put your dick back inside me. I'm almost there." She ordered between muffled moans. She was starting to pant my name. I removed my fingers and shoved my cock back inside her, grabbing her hips again shoving it in as far as possible. I pounded into her hard and fast and I could feel myself exploding as she tried to muffle her orgasm. I cried out as I emptied myself deep inside her, spots entering my vision. I leaned down over her taut body recovering from the dizziness.

After a few moments, she said that we needed to get back to the party. We both dressed hurriedly. We planned that I would leave ahead of her and in a few moments, she would follow. I put myself back together still in dreamland over what just happened. I opened the door to her bedroom to leave and looked back at her.

"That was better than winning the soccer championship." I walked back to the party, leaving her smiling in agreement.

8 THE ROGUE FATHER

My friend sits beside me on the plane, her nose buried deep in a romance book. I can't help thinking about how the hot guy on the cover looks so much like her dad – an image I am sure she wouldn't appreciate. I have had a crush on her dad since freshman year. He was tall, ruggedly handsome, and was in amazing shape. I couldn't believe that he was old enough to be my own father because he looked like an older brother.

It was sad that he was single. He shouldn't be since he was so attractive, but as my friend Elizabeth said, he didn't feel the need to get into a long term relationship. He had lost his wife fifteen years earlier and had raised my friend since then. That made him even more attractive to me.

I couldn't help the smile that spread across my face as I saw him waving to us when we got off of the plane. He looked as amazing as he did the last time I saw him. He gave Elizabeth a big hug and turned to me, pulling me into his embrace. I couldn't help the warmth that crept over me as I breathed in his musky scent. His arms were strong and I felt safe in his embrace.

As he broke the hug, he grinned and asked, "How are my girls?"

We both started talking his ear off about classes and our graduation, which was coming up in only a few short months. He navigated the streets with ease and before I even realized it, we were pulling into the large estate that they called home. He was very successful in business, which showed in the dark, pin striped suit that was tailored perfectly to fit him.

After he unloaded our luggage, he helped Elizabeth up to her room and then showed me to mine, which was across the house from hers. "I converted two of the guestrooms in the other wing into a home gym, now it is just the guestrooms in this wing that are free. I hope you don't mind."

"No, not at all. I kind of like being a little out of the way," I say as I walk closely beside him.

When he shows me my room, I can't help but smile at how far out of the way it was. All I needed to do was entice him back to my room and no one else in the house would hear my screams as I made love to him. His gaze lingers over me and I can't help but see the hunger in the depths of his eyes. There is no doubt that he wants me as much as I want him, I just need to give him a little nudge.

"Dinner will be at seven," he says before he closes the door and I am left to ponder my next move.

A little before seven, I find myself standing in front of the mirror, checking my appearance. I look so much older than my twenty two years. My black hair falls down my shoulders in ringlets and my blue eyes are a striking contrast to it. My skin is ivory and flawless and my ample cleavage shows perfectly in the strapless sundress I am wearing. It is tight and short, showing off my long legs.

I leave the room and head to the dining room. He is standing alone, a glass of wine in his hand. His eyes devour me as I walk in and I am turned on at the thought of him watching me. He pours me a glass of red wine and hands it to me. I watch him as I take a slow sip and I lick the sweet wine from my lips. His nostrils flare and he looks like he is going to say something when Elizabeth walks into the room.

"Hope I am not late for dinner, Daddy," she says.

"No Liz, I think you are just in time," he says using her nickname.

I try not to scowl at my friend. I really am happy to see her but I would have loved a few extra minutes with her dad. We all sit down at the table as the first course is served. He talks about his business and a few overseas ventures. Liz and I talk about our trip to Italy, which is planned for right after graduation.

After dinner, we take our wine out to the veranda. I sit across from him as Liz snuggles up against her dad. His eyes roam over my long legs and I shift to give him the best view of them. She yawns against him, her eyes sliding shut before she shakes herself.

"Daddy, I think jet lag is getting to me, I'm going to turn in."

He kisses the top of her head. "Okay sweetie, I will see you in the morning."

She yawns again and heads into the house after wishing me goodnight. Alone at last, I gaze at him. His eyes narrow and he focuses on my cleavage.

"Don't feel like you have to entertain this old man," he says and I can tell he is giving me a way out.

But I don't want a way out. I want his cock thrusting into me. My body is humming with need. "Do you have any music?" I ask.

He nods and moves to the stereo off to the side. He turns on some soft instrumental music. He turns back to me and I stand up, my movements sinewy as I sway towards him. "Dance with me," I murmur.

He shakes his head but I slide into his arms and we are dancing together. I can feel his hard shaft against my hip and I know that he wants me as desperately as I want him. I place a kiss on his neck and feel him stiffen but he doesn't push me away.

I place another kiss higher up and then another until I am kissing his jaw. Then, finally, my lips slide over his. I kiss him softly, then harder and with more urgency. The tension in my body is building and just the touch of his mouth is enough to bring me close to climax.

He growls as I slide my tongue into his mouth and then he pushes me away violently. I hit the veranda wall, a small cry escaping my mouth as I do. He shushes me and then he is on me. He is so strong, he rips apart my dress and the ruined material falls to the ground. I am not wearing a bra and he forces his knee between my legs as his hands massage my breasts. He licks the nipple and sucks it into his mouth. His teeth nip at my sensitive flesh and I find myself writhing on his knee, trying to feel some relief from the wanton need that is burning through me.

He twists my panties between his hands and rips off them off. I am so hot and wet that I am sure I will come right there as his fingers slide between my folds. He rubs my clit and I scream in delight right before his finger slides into me. He shushes me for a second time, but I am so hot and wet for him my body aches. I'm ready to take his cock into me.

I fumble with his pants and manage to get them off of his hips as his finger continues to stroke deep inside me. Then his fingers are replaced by his hard cock as he thrusts deeply into me. I wrap my legs around his waist as he braces me against the wall. He thrusts into me again and my need turns fiery. I bite his neck, begging for him to fuck me hard as he lifts me up by my ass and drops me down again and again on his cock.

I cry out and his hand covers my mouth, trying to quiet me. My tightness clenches his shaft as I feel him shudder deep within me. He holds me in place for a few moments, continuing to thrust as he unloads himself inside me. When he is done, he leans down and whispers in my ear,

"Thank you."

He releases me, both of us looking around for Liz or a member of the house staff and trying to put ourselves back together. Taking another satisfied breath I wrap my arms around his neck and kiss him deeply. Then I whisper into his ear, "If you want to thank me again, I'll be in my secluded room across the house where I don't have to be so quiet."

9 THE INNOCENT

The beat of the music was almost primal as the other college students swayed on the dance floor. Their movements made it look like they were caught up in love making. The song spoke of sex and passion and I found myself searching the door of the club again. She has to be here soon.

Danielle had promised to go out with us tonight, just me and a half dozen of our classmates. It wasn't a date, but it was the first time in over a year that she has actually said yes. I had been in to her since we first met in our psych class, but she had evaded my courtship. Instead, she had firmly placed me in the "friend" zone.

It was frustrating to say the least since I could tell that she was as attracted to me as I was to her. I would often find her staring at me in longing, whether it was in class, out with friends, or at the gym. I was completely in love with her.

A beautiful woman walked through the doors as I thought of Danielle. Her auburn hair hangs loose in long waves that reach the middle of her back, which was completely bare. A tight, red dress showed off her perfect form, the snug bodice forcing her breasts to spill over the top as she adjusts the short mini skirt. I groan as she raises her leg and I catch a glimpse of the six inch stilettos on her knee high, black leather, come-fuck-me boots.

She raises her tanned head and my mouth drops as I realize that the beauty is Danielle. She smiles at me, flashing her white teeth, and moves to greet me on the dance floor. She slips her arms around my waist and squeezes me hard as she hugs me. The smell of cherries wafts off of her and I bite back a groan as desire shoots straight to my groin.

I lean into her and inhale her deeply before I say, "Can I ask you something tonight?"

She gazes up into my eyes and as her lips form around a word, the music stops and our friends surround us.

"Danielle, you made it!"

I growl at their horrible timing and allow Jessica to pull Danielle to the booth. Her boyfriend, Derek, gives me an apologetic look and follows after her. At the table, we order drinks and as the couples break off to dance.

"Do you want to dance?" I query.

She nods and I take her hand as she slides out of the booth. Her bare skin burns under my hands as we grind together. I can feel my erection growing as we rub against each other. I can tell from the way her eyes are glowing that she knows exactly what she is doing to me. Her candy red lips beckon to me, but as I lean down to kiss her, she pulls away and walks back to the table.

Coming up behind her, I hear Jessica say, "You look so beautiful tonight Danielle. And the way you were dancing with Jacob was freaking hot."

"Yeah, why aren't you two together?" Derek adds.

Danielle doesn't say anything so I say with a wink, "Believe me, I've been working on it for a year. I think I'm wearing her down." I turn to Danielle, "Hey, you want to head to the VIP area to talk?"

She nods again and slips her hand into mine, pulling

me after her as she walks up the stairs. I can't help but to look under her dress, it is just too short to avoid, and I can see the red, lace panties peeking out from her hemline. I curse myself for taking her somewhere quiet.

We slide into the booth, set up in a dark corner with high backs for privacy. I lean back in the seat and order another round of drinks for us. "You do look beautiful tonight, why the change?"

She raises a slim shoulder in a shrug and says, "I just felt like a change. You look great tonight too."

I smile and shake my head. I look my usual self. My strong legs are encased in jeans and my black polo shirt is tight against my athletic abdomen. I had simply brushed my dark hair to the side and I knew it looked tousled. I grin at her anyways and before I realize it, we are right back into the friend zone. Chatting about classes, her family and what she plans on doing in the summer. As we talk, I drink, but I can't help noticing that she is ordering water and taking longer than me to finish our drinks.

Still, I say nothing about it and simply enjoy the laughter that we are sharing. I notice her looking at my groin now and then, licking her lips. She is definitely attracted to me. After a while, the laughter suddenly stops and she is standing in front of me. She slides onto my lap, her short skirt riding up and I strain not to put my hands on her ass. She starts swinging her hips back and forth, riding my growing cock as she dances.

Turning around, she places her bare back against my chest and rubs her ass along the bulge in my pants. I can't get over how hot this lap dance is and I let her place my hands on her hips, guiding her rubbing. There is no doubt that she knows exactly what she is doing to me. I begin panting and I can feel my cock spasm. I find it hard to breathe and I gently push her off of me.

"I have to go to the bathroom," I manage before I get up and rush to the washroom.

Inside, I take several calming breathes. I was seconds away from blowing my load. Splashing cold water into my face, I look at my hazel eyes in the mirror. "Get it together buddy. She is giving you all the signals. You can do this...stop thinking you will ruin this...you have wanted her for over a year."

As I am finishing my pep talk, Derek walks in. "There you are," his brow furrows with concern. "You okay man?"

I laugh, "Yeah, never better. Were you looking for me?"

"Yeah, Danielle got me and said she feels sick. She was wondering if you could walk her home."

Excitement courses through me and I rush out of the bathroom. Concern floods through me when I find her and I check her over. She looks flushed but other than that, she doesn't look too sick.

"Are you okay? I'll walk you home."

I drape my leather coat over her shoulders and guide her from the bar. We spend the short walk to her townhouse talking and we ignore the elephant in the room...or specifically, the way she had been dancing on my lap.

When we reach her house, I kiss her forehead and take a step back, the words on my lips to ask her out again. She bites her lip, appearing to be uncertain before she says, "Do you want to come in for a drink?"

I grin, "Sure, if you feel up to it."

Reaching her living room, I take a seat on her couch as she walks into the kitchen. She emerges with two beers and says, "Thanks for walking me home; you're such a good friend."

I sigh at her word, I don't want to be friends. She passes me the beer and then moves towards the window. She closes the blinds and turns back to me, her eyes blazing. "But I have something to confess...I wasn't sick, I just wanted to get you alone. I can't control what I feel any longer. I want to be more than just friends."

She sets her beer down and slowly slides the straps of her dress off. I stand up and grab her hands. Searching her face, I ask, "Are you sure you want to do this?"

Her laughter is throaty and it sends all the blood rushing to my dick. "God yes," she shakes her hand to free my grip and continues to slide the dress off, "I have been waiting a year to do this."

She strips off her dress and turns away from me. Looking back over her shoulder, she says, "Well, are you coming?"

I grin and follow her scantily clad ass. She isn't wearing a bra so her tight breasts swing as she walks and the red panties are beckoning to me as I strip my clothes, following her. She looks brave as she walks; but I wonder if she is feeling the fear I am suddenly feeling. Maybe she won't go through with this because she will be afraid of ruining our friendship.

As I reach the bedroom, I find her standing in front of the bed. I suck in my breath at her beauty. She has removed her panties; a small dusting of auburn hair covers the apex of her thighs. She is wearing nothing but those sexy boots. She gasps as I draw closer and I find her staring at my groin, eyes wide. I feel a sense of pride at her reaction but I wonder at the small amount of fear that has crossed her eyes.

I move into her and lift her chin. Placing a tender kiss on her lips, I avoid touching her naked body although I really want to press my length into her. She sighs on my kiss and her lips open slightly. I take the invitation and delve deeply in her mouth.

She melts against me and I feel seared by her touch before she pulls away and takes a step back. I feel a moment of panic that she is going to say no after all. She looks so scared and so innocent standing there in front of me. She opens her mouth to speak, stops and then starts again, "Jacob, there is something I need to tell you before we go any farther."

Concern causes me to take a step towards her and she retreats a step back, putting her hands up to stop me. "I have wanted to tell you for a long time but I couldn't."

I take a step back and wait for her to finish. She takes a deep breath and the words rush out of her, "I have never been with anyone before."

I am dumbstruck for a moment. How could I have not known? I was her friend and I never realized just how innocent she was. I feel honored that she is offering this part of herself to me. My heart swells and I almost stop.

Moving forward, I lift her up and place her gently on the bed. I remove her come-fuck-me boots and she looks at me questioningly. I chuckle and say, "Fucking comes later. Tonight I'm going to make love to you."

I lean down on her and kiss her full lips. She sighs into me and I kiss along her jaw, going further until her breasts are spilling over my hands. I place a kiss on the tight kernel of her nipple, she moans under me, and I suck it into my mouth, gently teasing the flesh until she is thrashing under me.

I move down her body, placing kisses on her stomach, her hips, her thighs. Nudging her legs open, I sniff and sigh at how wonderful she smells. I separate her folds tenderly with my fingers and lean in to place a gentle lick against her slit before I turn my mouth to her clit and work it between my lips. She thrashes on the bed, crying out my name as I spear my tongue into her tight entrance. I can feel her wetness and her climax building, so I move back up the length of her, kissing as I do. I want her to feel cherished.

Bringing my cock to her virgin passage, I pause and stare down into her eyes. "Are you sure?"

She pulls me down and kisses me, sliding her tongue over my lips. Breaking the kiss, she breathes, "God yes. Make love to me Jacob."

Not needing any other encouragement, I slowly press my cock inside her. I feel her barrier stretch before my cock and I feel her stiffen in pain as I break through it. I kiss her forehead and her jaw. Stilling completely, I'm buried to the hilt inside her as her body adjusts to my size. I take turns taking her nipples into my mouth.

As she starts to moan and make small movements under me, I reach down and start playing with her clit and start thrusting inside of her. Gently at first and then with more urgency as we both ache desperately for our release. As she tightens around my cock, I feel her shudder her release and I capture her screams of ecstasy with my kiss. With my full weight on her I fall over the edge as I thrust again and again without thought as my cock jerks once, twice and then my load comes shooting out of me, deep into her.

Recovering slowly, I finally push up onto my hands to let her breathe. I look down at her face, which is rosy from our love making, and lean down to kiss her. As I break the kiss, with my cock still buried deep inside her, I say, "I was going to ask you out on a date at the beginning of this night, but now I can't." I watch her brow crease in curiosity then I add, "Marry me instead." Happiness shines through her eyes as she pulls me into a fierce hug, my cock twitching back to life inside her.

10 THE ATHLETE

Smoothing down my gray slacks, I glance around at the other reporters sitting in the waiting room. The majority of them are men and only five of the thirty reporters, including myself, are women. I sigh. There just aren't a lot of female sports reporters out there, which is why I have tried to make myself look decidedly unfeminine in my tailored gray slacks, white blouse and dark, horn rimmed glasses. Everything screams professional, the way the clothes hide my hourglass figure and large breasts. Even my long, auburn waves are caught up in a tight bun to make me seem more like a jock than a jock's wet dream.

This is what I do to get into these rooms. I have been interviewing athletes for well over five years and I realized early on that appearing like a guy got me into more places, places like the Olympic training center where I was waiting to interview several of the multi-event athletes.

"Ms. Aubry, please come this way." A non-descript man wearing sports pants and shirt says to me.

I nod, gather up my satchel and pull out a pen and pad from it before I follow the man into the dressing room. Standing beside a locker, in nothing but a tight pair of shorts that clearly show off his large, and I mean large, anatomy, is the object of my fantasies...er...I mean my interview, Brandon Carter. He is magnificent, his wide shoulders tapering down to a trim, six pack stomach and his chest is as hard and chiselled as his square jaw and high cheekbones. His dark hair is damp and dripping down his face and his blue eyes look me over me in interest.

I quickly avert my eyes, something I had trained myself to do long ago, but from the wry smile, I know he saw my interested appraisal. "So, where do you want to begin?" He asks, his smooth, southern drawl curling my toes as he does.

"Umm," I say, completely flustered. I want to tell him how magnificent he is, how I would love to cup his dick and feel its weight in my hands, but I shake those thoughts from my head. It would be completely unprofessional and would get me barred from dressing rooms for life. Not something a sports reporter can afford.

"How well do you think training is coming?" I finally say, trying to gather my thoughts.

He sits down on the bench, and stares at my breasts as he does. I feel exposed under his perusal and I can feel heat spreading out from my breasts...almost like his hands were there. "Good, my timing is off on the 5000, but I'll get there."

"Do you think that your injury last year is affecting your stamina?"

His eyes narrow but a slow grin spreads across his lush lips and I almost sigh. "No, my stamina is fine. I can go for hours."

I feel a blush rising to my cheeks and I am positive that he is speaking about more than the 5000. I run through a dozen other questions about his expectations, making the Olympic team and where he thinks he will place at the Olympics. Brock answers them with ease, each question filled with a hidden innuendo and by the time I am done, I want to reach down and feel his sweaty skin.

"So are we done?"

The question draws me out of the trance I was in and I

realize that I have been staring for too long. I nod my head sadly, but as I am closing my notebook, I say quickly, "For now, but I may have other questions. Could I call you if I have any follow up?"

Crap, why am I asking this? I chide myself silently, then hear him ask, "Or maybe we could go for a drink tonight and I could ask you some questions?" His eyes twinkle as his grin deepens.

"Sure, that sounds good." I stammer.

"Great, why don't you come by my house and you can finish the interview there?"

He stands up, grabs the pen from my numb fingers, and jots down his address. Before I know it, I am standing outside with my interview done and a date for that evening.

****

Waiting for the door to open, I smooth my hand down the clingy, purple shift dress that I wore for the evening. It matched the deep purple bra and panties underneath and made it feel like I was wearing nothing at all. Glancing at my reflection in the window, I grin at the waves of auburn hair cascading down my back and the tasteful makeup that completes the look. The purple stilettos tie everything together, but I kept my glasses on...maybe in an effort to keep things professional.

My breathe catches when Brandon opens the door, his wide chest completely exposed, the open dress slacks hanging on his waist. I lick my lips and his smile beckons to me. "Ms. Aubry, please come in. Sorry that you caught me like this, I was late getting back from the training center and I'm still getting dressed."

Heat flushes my cheeks and I am positive my eyes are filled with lust as I enter his modernly furnished house. I follow him, admiring the way his muscles move as he walks to a sitting room at the back of the house. Wall to ceiling windows give the perfect view of a pool and the city beyond. A fire glows in the large fireplace on one side of the room.

"If you'll excuse me, I'll go and finish getting dressed," he says as he slips out of the room.

I glance around the large space before moving to the windows. The city lights sparkle like diamonds below us and the water from the pool beckons. I hear him clear his throat behind me and turn around. He is resting against the bar, his pants done up and a dress shirt hanging open from his shoulders. He watches me, heat filling his eyes. Pouring two glasses of red wine, he hands me one and beckons me over to the couch, "Why don't you take off your shoes and get comfortable for the interview?"

I nod, slip the heels from my feet, and slide into the micro suede black couch facing the fireplace. Tucking my legs under me, I smooth my skirt and then fish out my pen and pad. I clear my throat as he slides onto the couch beside me and gives me a wink.

"So," I twirl my pen, "how are you feeling about your team?"

His eyes linger over my cleavage, which is on full display with this dress, before he answers. "I am really happy with them. They are a group of talented athletes. I think we will medal."

"Just medal?"

"Well, I am sure we will win gold, I mean, I always slide across that finish line in good time."

His eyes move to my groin and I wonder if he can sense how hard my clit is throbbing. I run through a number of other questions, slowly sipping the wine as I try to gather my thoughts. He answers them all, each one alluding to the way he could play my body.

His hand reaches out and gathers up a long lock of my hair. As he talks, his fingers twirl it around his hand and he begins to slide his fingers along my neck. I shudder and fight down the urge to slide my fingers over his bare chest, which is peaking out of his open shirt. Remain calm Aubry, don't give in to him. I repeat the words to myself over and over as he leans over and breathes me in.

I shudder as he kisses my neck, gooseflesh jumping up on my skin. His tongue traces a line up my skin to my ear where he begins to suck the lobe. I bite back the groan as liquid fire moves through my body and hits down below. I've craved this all day.

Slipping the notepad from my hand, he lays it on the floor before holding his hand out to me. I take it and allow him to draw me up out of my seat and lead me to a spot in front of the fire. He leans in and captures my mouth and my hands splay across his chest. I feel like his skin is branding me, making me yearn for more.

His hands slide down to my hemline and he lifts the dress up and over me. He drops lower and runs kisses along my stomach and over my breasts as my hands dig into his scalp, tangling into his hair. Pulling my bra free, he sucks at one nipple before sliding his tongue over to the next. My panties slide off of me at his urging and I melt to the bear skin rug along with him.

Capturing his head, I draw his face up to mine where I run my tongue over his lip, urging him to open to me. When he does, I kiss him hard, licking up the taste of him. My hands remove his clothing as I lick and bite and suck his mouth. Breaking free of the kiss, I run my hands over the hard muscles of his chest and stomach. I slowly move up to his arms and then slide my hands over his ass. I take in the silky texture of him before I wrap my fingers around his thick, large manhood.

Pushing him to his back, I run my lips down his body and lick the salty drop of liquid forming at the tip of him. He groans and his hips thrust towards me. I smile and slowly swallow his huge cock, my hands fisting around the base of his shaft as I take him as far as I can. I run my mouth up and down his shaft, sucking him as his cock jumps in my mouth.

"Enough," he growls out before flipping me onto the carpet on my back. The soft fur tickling my skin as he starts biting me lightly. He works a trail of kisses and bites from my neck to my breasts and then he works them over. Torturing my hard nipples with gentle nips before soothing the teased flesh with his tongue, he sucks my nipple into his mouth and I arch toward him.

Chuckling, he explores lower and when he reaches my pussy, he pauses before his tongue flicks out and thrusts into me. I scream in ecstasy and allow him to lick deep in me, calling out his name as he does. He sucks in my clit and I gasp, "I need you now!"

With barely a pause, he is nestled between my legs, his huge cock sliding up my slit before he thrusts into me. I groan at how large he is, but I grip his ass, urging him to go deeper. He thrusts into me, harder each time. Tension builds in my body with each thrust and I feel dizzy each time he withdraws from me. I wrap my legs around his waist and arch my back meeting him stroke for stroke as lights dance in my head.

His hand grasps my breast and his thumb rubs my nipple – sending tremors of passion through my body as his other hand makes his way down and rubs my clit. I feel myself vibrating and then the dam comes crashing down and I am crying out, begging him not to stop. I can feel the liquid flowing from me as it spasms around him; over and over again it tightens against him in my climax.

He grinds his teeth, his thrusting harder and faster each time I quiver around him and with a final drive into me, he roars and I feel him release inside me.

Falling forward thoroughly drained he catches his breath. As my thoughts start to come back to me, he leans down, his breath harsh and teasing in my ears as he asks, "Will there be any other questions?"

11 THE LANDSCAPER

It had taken me nearly eight months of planning and work but my yard had slowly been transformed from the desert wasteland full of weeds that it had been to the lush garden that it was now. I sighed at the beauty and loved what the landscaper had done.

I had watched him over the months as he worked a miracle on my yard but it wasn't just because I enjoyed the sight of my garden taking shape. It was partly because of how hot my landscaper was.

The first time I had met him, I was instantly attracted to him. He had short hair that was bleached blonde from all the hours working in the sunshine, his green eyes were filled with laughter and his body was hard and trim. But as sexy as his body was, it was his passion for landscaping that made my panties wet. I had spent nearly three months deciding on the design just so I could spend hours bantering with him. I had finally decided on a fifty percent hardscape garden complete with an outside bed and reflection pool.

Then it had been another five months of watching him direct his crew and lift rock after rock, his bare chest glistening with sweat under the hot sun as he spread the gravel and laid the small amount of sod. I had to have daily showers just to cool the desire racing through my body.

Today though, I felt completely disappointed. My garden was done and while it was beautiful, it meant I wouldn't be seeing my landscaper any more. He had assistants that maintained the work. I had dressed special for this walk through to appraise the work. My silk sundress was little more than a negligee with its thin straps and clingy fabric that ended mid-thigh. I didn't care; I wanted him to look at me the way I had been looking for the last eight months. I even ignored my much needed bra so my breasts were straining at the ties, trying to get out.

As we walked through the garden, I couldn't come up with any changes to keep him working for me longer. I told him how beautiful everything was and I couldn't help but smile when I found his eyes hovering on my breasts or focused on my ass. I was positive he could see the outline of my thong through the fabric.

At the reflecting pool, I sigh.

"Is something wrong?"

"No, just thinking about how beautiful it is now." I turn and look deeply into his eyes, urging him to see the fiery little vixen that I could be. My brown hair was cascading down my back and my skin was soft and smooth from the lotion I had rubbed on it. "And I was thinking how much I will miss you."

He doesn't say anything, just nods as he starts checking off the final items on his clipboard. "You know," he says slowly and his voice wraps around me, causing my body to flare, "I have you down for monthly maintenance and I would be happy to come out and see to it myself."

I squeal in delight, unable to stop myself and he glances up at me in alarm, "That would be wonderful, but there is something else I need you to do for me."

"Really? What would that be? I'm pretty sure that I did everything according to your blueprint."

I saunter up to him, swinging my hips as I do. I pull the clipboard from his hands and purr, "I need you to fuck me."

I kiss him deeply and pull his body tight against me. My teeth bite at his lip, urging him to open for me and he does as he wraps his arms around me. Then his tongue is invading my mouth and I realize that he has taken control of the kiss. The lust in his embrace makes me ache and I can feel his hands cupping my ass, playfully running his fingertips under the hem of my dress.

I push him back toward the retaining wall and slip his t-shirt off, kissing the taught flesh like I have wanted to do for months. He growls in frustration as my teeth graze his nipples and suddenly his hands on my ass aren't playful anymore as he slides my dress up and over my head. He sends it flying and I brace my hands on his shoulders as he cups my breasts and nips at them.

His eyes are dark with need. "I have wanted to suck these for months," and suddenly, he is sucking my nipple into his mouth.

I cry out and plunge my hands into his hair, pulling on the short lengths as he moves back and forth from nipple to nipple. My panties are soaking wet when he moves down my stomach, kissing and licking the smooth expanse. The breeze on my nipples sends tendrils of desire through me and I groan as he presses a thumb to my clit.

He picks me up and heads for the outside bed he built with his own hands and lays me down on the firm cushion. He slides my thong down and nudges my legs apart. I brace my hands on his shoulders as his tongue plunges up into me. I can't help the gush of liquid that escapes from my womanhood, but he moans in pleasure and begins lapping it up. His thumb works my clit as his tongue plunges into me again and again, each time he moans out his excitement and it shudders through me.

I feel my knees weaken as the tension builds in my body and I pull his hair, unable to help myself. He moves his mouth to my clit and sucks it between his teeth, biting it lightly. Light flashes behind my closed eyes and I am screaming out in my orgasm as he allows me to lie there and recover.

He sheds his jeans, his cock jumping at its freedom and moves around until it is bobbing above me. I reach for it and pump it several times before I maneuver it into my entrance.

He thrust hard and deep and my legs shake from the pleasure of him in my tight folds. When he is buried to the hilt, I wait as my body adjusts to his size and I can see from his face that he is enjoying just being sheathed inside me.

When he begins to groan, I begin to move, rocking my hips back and forth as I grind on his cock. His hands move to my waist and I feel him take control. His fingers bite into my flesh as he pulls me up and down on his cock, harder and faster.

My breasts swing at the movement and I reach up and grasp one, pinching the nipple as he rides me while the other hand strokes my clit. He drives faster and deeper, moaning louder and I find myself moaning with him as the tension builds inside. Then he thrusts one final time upward and I feel my body coming apart as I cry out, shaking with another orgasm. I am vaguely aware of him crying out with me as he reaches his own, his cock jerking and emptying inside me.

Taking a deep breath, I glance around at my beautiful garden and then back to this amazing man. I lean up, plant a kiss to his ear and say, "Sign me up for weekly maintenance instead."

12 THE BEST FRIEND

Her lips pressed against mine, tentatively at first and then with an urgency that surprised me. It's the first time I have ever kissed a girl. I stood there for a moment, breathing in her scent – the peach Schnapps from her cocktail, her cherry lip gloss, and her vanilla body wash. She was like a fruit salad and her lips were as delicious as I had always imagined.

Around us, dancers swayed to the music and I was positive that we were receiving a few surprised stares from the people that we knew, but I didn't care; all I cared about was the woman kissing me. Her small hands brushed along my full breasts, making them seem even larger than they were as she playfully flicked my pebbled nipple. I gasped, giving her the opportunity to slip her tongue into my mouth.

I sucked on her tongue, drawing her deeper, my own hands digging into her ass as we made out. I wanted this woman who was the complete opposite of me, dark haired, with her light green eyes and ivory skin that was at odds against my dusty complexion, blonde hair and brown eyes. Where I had always felt ordinary, she had been exotic. She was vivacious and carefree and she could blend in to any class of people she wanted to.

She drew me out, kept me from being shy. Just like she was doing now as her tongue tangled with mine and her hands cupped my breasts. Her moans of pleasure wrapping up into our own erotic world on the dance floor...

"Jess?"

The voice drew me from the memory of that night. Shaking myself from the image of Mila, I say, "Sorry, Mila. I kind of zoned out there for a minute."

Mila's sigh made me blush. Even though we had shared that moment together, the same moment I had been reliving for the last week since it happened, Mila didn't remember it. She had been drunk, she wasn't being herself, and while my body ached to see where that wild kiss could take us, our friendship meant too much to me to toss it away for sex. She was my oldest friend, one I have known since college and I couldn't ruin it.

"Are you as excited as I am?"

I stare out the window of the limo and try to gather my thoughts. Even though I had tried to fight it, Mila had convinced me to go to a club with her. The Masquerade, it was called. Everyone wore masks and women wore long maroon robes to conceal their identity. I had never even heard of it before but Mila seemed to have her thumb on the pulse of latest entertainment; probably had everything to do with her family's wealth.

"Yeah, a little," I lie.

"Well, you don't look it." Her green eyes narrow as she considers me. Raising a glass filled with champagne, she hands me another and gently clicks them together, "To an evening that will open our eyes," she says cryptically.

Before I can have a chance to reply, my mouth drops at the sight of the large castle. Dozens of people are waiting at the front gates of the castle as the dark clouds, threatening rain, hide the majority of the building from sight. It must look magical during the day, I think to myself, as I down the champagne in my glass, questioning this castle as a "club."

Taking a deep breath, I follow Mila out of the car and past the crowd waiting to get inside. She brushes past the doorman with a smile and into a large room where an attendant dressed in a black robe and a silver mask reaches for her invitation. Following the attendant, I glance around the room at the rich, gold brocade and expensive furniture that including a seating area.

Leaving us in a room with two long, maroon robes, the attendant walks away and I realize that I couldn't tell if was a man or a woman who had lead us around the room. The door clicks shut quietly and Mila turns toward me, mischief clear on her face.

"Take off everything you are wearing, except your panties and bra, and slip on the robe and mask," she passes me my robe, which feels like pure silk.

I shrug, not bothering to question her instructions and slip off the Band-Aid dress that I was wearing. I sigh in relief that I am wearing matching black lace panties and bra with matching nylons and garters. I slip the robe over my head and almost sigh at the cool fabric. I glance in the mirror and watch Mila slip her robe on, admiring the athletic build that is so different from my curves.

"Here, let me get the hood," she says and I allow her to slide the hood over my blonde hair. Gazing in the mirror, I realize that there is no way to know who we are and I wonder why the club does this.

Taking a deep breath, I follow Mila out of the room into a large ballroom. Tables line the sides of the room while a DJ takes up the entire one wall of the room. In the center is a large dance floor with robed people gyrating to the music. The beat of the song pulses into me and I feel heat spread through my body. The room is packed and I would guess about two hundred people are in the room, women masked and robed in maroon and men masked and robed in black. I gaze into the hoods of everyone we pass, but if I know anyone in the room, I have no idea who it is. I lean over Mila's shoulder to exclaim "This is awesome! I bet this place is full of secrets."

Snatching two glasses of champagne from a robed attendant, she shoves one into my hand and says, "Are you ready to see the rest?"

I nod, not sure if I am ready, but something about the press of people makes me want to venture somewhere else. Mila leads us through two large, wooden doors and down a short hallway. It is almost a labyrinth that she takes me through – her hand firmly gripping mine as she drags me behind her. I can feel her excitement and it starts to catch. Heat pulses between my legs and a blush creeps up my neck at the need that Mila's innocent touch is creating in me.

We enter a dimly lit room and I gasp at the sight. The room is filled with people having sex, men with women, women with men, women with women, even a woman with two men – all of them grinding against each other, groaning and panting in various stages of orgasm. The sounds buffet against me and I feel a gush of wetness at the apex of my thighs. I pull back slightly, not sure if I should go on or if we should turn back. Mila glances back, her eyes flashing in challenge as she grips my hand tighter and pulls me forward.

We walk the length of the room, stopping now and then to watch the lovers in their play. A large breasted woman, her robe half off, bent over a leather sofa as a man pounds into her. Her shrieks of pleasure cause more heat to pool between my legs and I can feel my clit throbbing in time to their lovemaking. Mila and I stand there, watching them fuck, her breasts swaying with each thrust, his large hand slapping her ass as she begs him for more.

Champagne glasses keep entering my hand from some unnoticed attendant and I am draining my second before I realize it. My own need beats at me and the trepidation about being here is gone. Now all I want to do is continue watching. All I want is someone to touch my clit and release the tension building there.

I startle as I realize that that is exactly what is happening. Mila has reached around me and slipped my robe open at the front. Her hand reaches down and presses my clit through my panties. I still my body, waiting for her to make the next move, loving the contact of her fingers running up and down my panties, teasing my clit until I am panting under her.

Removing her hand, she pulls me back towards a couch. Her mouth teases at my ear. "Sit down Jess."

I groan, but do exactly what she is telling me to do. As I sit down, she pushes me to lean back against the soft cushions and slides my robe completely open to expose my breasts. Her soft hands pull my knees apart and she drops to her knees in front of me. I take in her bright, passion-filled eyes but she shakes her head, "Watch the couple," she commands and my eyes flick up to the man and woman fucking on the couch across from us.

I notice that they are now watching us, just like we are watching them, and a small crowd has gathered to watch us. A part of me wants to cover up but as her fingers return to my clit, rubbing it in slow circles, that part is burned away by the liquid fire flowing through me. Mila pulls my bra down, freeing my aching breasts before her tongue laves one nipple. She gently grazes it with her teeth before she sucks it into her mouth swirling her tongue around it in the same lazy motion that her thumb is swirling over my clit.

Switching to my other breast, she sucks the nipple into her mouth as her hands hook my underwear under her thumbs. She slowly slides them away and I lift my hips to allow her. I can hear moans rising and falling around me and I realize that I am moaning with them, feeding off the eroticism of their voices as Mila's capable tongue strokes my flesh and sends me close to orgasm.

Her lips break from my skin and my nipples burn with need. She gives me a wicked grin, her tongue slipping between my lips as she licks deeply into my mouth. All I can taste is her cherry lip gloss and champagne and I reach to pull her down on me. She breaks the kiss and shakes her head, again, giving me that wicked grin before she drops down to her knees once more.

Her eyes burn into mine as she flicks her tongue over my clit and I jerk at the sensation, but her hand splays over my stomach, holding me in place. She flicks it again before she sucks my clit into her mouth. I scream in ecstasy, my body shaking as my orgasm continues to grow with each suck. Her one hand holds me down and she runs the fingers of her other hand over my slit. Inserting one finger inside me, she begins to thrust it back and forth as her tongue sucks and licks my clit.

I am bucking under her, my hands twisting in her dark silky hair. She lifts her head and says, "Watch the couple fucking, Jess. Watch them while I fuck you."

Burying her head back into my pussy, she returns to licking and sucking, her finger sliding in and out of me as the man's cock slides in and out of the woman. I watch them, struggling to keep my eyes open as they fuck and watch me, moving at the same speed as Mila between my legs. As I hear the man roar out in orgasm, I follow and begin screaming and bucking at the same time. My orgasm ripping me apart as Mila laps up the juices flowing from my center.

I feel completely alive, every nerve dancing in ecstasy as the spasms start to subside. This is the first orgasm I have ever had and I can barely forge a complete thought as Mila rises up to kiss me. I can taste myself on her lips and I find myself licking her clean. As I finish, I can hear the sound of applause and I hear Mila whisper in my ear, "Your secret is safe with me."

13 THE HIGH SCHOOL SWEETHEART

The sound of the 90's music filled the room and I had to shudder at my revulsion. I didn't want to be here and had sworn that the last time anyone here would see me was at graduation 20 years ago.

Despite all the crap I had put up with from the jocks at the school, I had become more than just some nerd. I was extremely successful after launching my own social networking site. I had more money than I could ever want after another social networking site bought me out. My weak build was gone and was replaced by the body of an athlete. I looked good in my Armani suit and I even had a full head of hair, which I still wore a little long.

I could see the old high school cheerleaders murmuring to each other as they checked me out. Some of them were still hot, but they didn't interest me. Instead, I was looking for the dark beauty that had haunted me since she had dumped me at senior prom. Lorna was the only reason why I was here. She was my high school sweetheart and we had gone our separate ways when we went to college.

I watched her across the room and longing shot through my groin. I was pleasantly surprised she was here – she was a famous actress after all, but I knew her secrets, she would always be the sweet girl next door with her tanned skin and ebony black hair.

She had the long tresses caught up in a loose bun and I could see her long neck. Her green eyes scanned the crowd lazily as people tried to get close to her. I avoided her gaze and moved towards the bar. I didn't want to talk to her...at least not yet.

Instead, I drank my beer and watched the high school "gods" relive their glory days. They had gone on to a mediocre life with a job at the local factory, a house, and a few kids. I smiled as my buddy Max found me at the bar. We had been best friends in school and often found ourselves at the receiving end of bullying.

"Hey James," he said in way of greeting, "You just get here?"

I shake my head, "No, I've been here for hours."

Laughing, he eyed me, "Sure you have. If you had, I'm sure you would be all over Lorna by now."

I laugh at the ease that we fell into. We actually did business a lot and I had maintained the friendship after we graduated. He was often my partner in crime when we went out drinking. I shrugged, but I could see the mass of people moving towards me. I knew in the center of that mass was Lorna.

Glancing at all the old yearbook photos on the wall, I ignore her as she leans in and kisses Max on the cheek. I can feel her staring at me but I refuse to meet her gaze. Her husky laugh finally draws my eyes to her and she says, "James, you were always good at keeping a low profile."

"Thanks. I wasn't planning on coming, but Max made me."

Her laughter rings through the air and I can't help but want her. She looked amazing in a tight bandage dress, the black fabric pulling snugly over her ample breasts. The stilettos on her feet brought her five foot ten height even with my six foot three frame. I wanted to reach out and pull her in for a kiss.

Instead, I stand up straight and smile at her. "It's good to see you Lorna. You look amazing." I lean in and place a kiss on her cheek, lingering there to breathe in her vanilla scent before I stand back.

But before I do, she whispers, "And you smell as good as you look."

Lightning shoots through me and I stare at her, not sure if I hear her right. Her smile turns wry and she gives me a wink. "I really think we should catch up James," her hand slides over my arm and I feel my skin prickle at her touch. "Why don't you order me a martini?"

I nod, "For you darling, I would order the world," I say as I slide my hand across her back. She shivers under my touch and I know that she is definitely still attracted to me.

As I order the drinks, I feel her hand on my back, running it up and down as she chats with the people around us. I feel a bit of irritation at these fake people. They had less to do with her than they did me when we were teens. Now that she is famous, they can't stop fawning over her. I slide the drink into her hand as she says, "Why don't we go for a walk to catch up?"

I grin as I look down at her shoes questionably. She follows my gaze, shrugs, and I let her lead me through the crowd. I hear a groan of complaint from the crowd but she ignores them and pulls me outside. Once we clear the door she takes off her shoes as we begin to walk. The dark football field spreads out from the gymnasium where the reunion is being held and that seemed to be our destination.

"Do you remember how we kissed for the first time under those bleachers?" Her eyes are filled with mischief as she waves towards the bleachers. "Oh, if this stadium could talk." She sighs.

I laugh, "I know, we did more than just kiss under there. If I remember right, you let me get to third base under those bleachers."

Her mock horror makes me laugh harder, "I do

declare, I would never have been such a floozy. You must be thinking of Sandy Jenkins."

The thought of the mousey girl wrinkles my nose, but I play with her, "Oh yeah, Sandy. Man, I remember how hot she was. Do you think she is here?"

She pushes me playfully as we walk towards the center of the fifty yard line. "Very funny, but you know you're mine."

I pause and she turns towards me. I can see her blush at the words that have slipped from her lips. She looks out at the football field. "So, do you come home often?"

Shaking my head, I shift my growing hardness to a more comfortable spot in my pants and say, "No, I haven't been back in about fifteen years – long enough to move my parents out to the coast when I bought them a house and since then, I have been too busy. I travel a lot for business, mostly overseas. You?" She doesn't answer me, but instead stares at the bleachers where I had rounded third.

She visibly shakes herself, "Me?"

"Yeah, do you come here often?" I grin, trying to break the serious mood that has come over her.

She grins back, "No, just today for this reunion. I really just wanted to find one specific person from my past and now I have."

Her gaze bores into me and she leans in, her breath heavy on my lips. She places a tentative kiss, like she is testing whether I will push her away or not. I groan and pull her into me, sliding my tongue into her mouth. I grind my hard shaft against her body and I hear her moan into my mouth.

Sweeping my hands down her back, I squeeze her ass and pull her up onto me. She straddles my waist and begins grinding her hot center against my bulge. Her bandage dress rides up high and I can feel that her ass is bare. I glance down between us and see that she is wearing a thong. "You came prepared," I purr.

"Always," she murmurs as she nips at my jaw and then runs her tongue along my neck. When she reaches my ear, she bites down gently and I almost come at the feel of her mouth.

I pull the bodice of her dress down and her breasts spring free. They are still small, and I'm grateful that she hasn't given in to the trend to get fake ones. Hers are perfect and the large erect nipple tastes delicious as I lick it like ice cream.

She arches her back to give me better access to her breasts and lap at the sweet flesh she offers me. She rubs against me as I nuzzle her breasts and I feel my orgasm building.

Still straddling my waist, I grab at her hips, drop to my knees, and still her moving body. She looks at me questioningly and I place my hand between us. My fingers slide into her wet slit and she begins rocking against my hand as I work her clit between my thumb and index finger.

I return to kissing and licking her breasts as she fucks my finger. I slide one finger inside her and feel her wetness sucking at my finger. I groan in excitement and she reaches between us, pulling my cock free. "Fuck me James," she pants out stroking my length.

I hold her in place and put her on her back with me on top of her. I tear the thin fabric of her panties off and before she can catch her breath, I plunge to the hilt inside her. I stop when I am completely buried, loving the feel of her throbbing against my cock.

Then we begin moving in tempo and it is like we had never broken up. I fit in her perfectly. She grinds on my cock, rocking her hips back and forth as my fingers continue to tease her clit. I let her control the speed and depth and I bite my cheek in an effort to hold off my orgasm.

As she bucks under me a final time, I hear her scream

my name out into the night and my own climax sends me thrusting harder and faster as my seed shoots deep inside her. I cry out myself and then we collapse together completely satisfied. She looks up to me, heat still evident in her eyes as we hear applause far off into the darkness. "So much for keeping a low profile." She teases me.

14 THE MASSEUSE

I stewed on my anger as I sat in the cab headed uptown. I was pissed that my day was being wasted on this trip but what choice did I have. Corporate business was my life and I enjoyed my work but with the newest merger, I had been a bit testy with everyone in my office, including my boss.

Today, when he had interrupted me, I had snapped at him and had come inches away from losing my job. He was not impressed and he ordered me to his office. His words were grim as he said, "Look John, you are the best in my firm but I will toss your ass to the curb if you ever do that again."

I had felt a little remorse at my outburst, but the man had been driving me crazy with a dozen different questions as we bought and sold off our latest company. Instead of coming up with an excuse, I swallowed my words as he pulled out a business card and tossed it to me.

"You go and see Lillian today or you're fired. You need to deal with the stress and anger you are feeling before you are back on the project."

My jaw dropped and I tried to argue with him about taking me off the project for a day. He ignored me and had his secretary set up the appointment with the masseuse.

So here I was, my tall six foot two frame folded into the backseat of a cab, my five o'clock shadow scratching my collar as I ground my perfect white teeth together. My boyish charm wasn't going to work on my boss so I had no choice but go to the masseuse. The card he had given me was shiny black with only an address on it.

The house we pulled up at looked more like a hotel and was quite large. I couldn't believe how well groomed the grounds were as I walked up to it and rang the doorbell. The door swung open and a butler wearing the finest clothing raised an eyebrow at me.

"I am here to see Lillian," I said.

"Yes, this way please."

He ushered me into the foyer and I whistled quietly. The house looked like it should be on one of those TV shows that showcases the homes of celebrities. Dark wood and intricate marble covered the decor. A grand staircase circled the large foyer and as I followed the plush carpet up the stairs, I watched a breathtaking brunette coming down the stairs. She smiled at me and held out her hand. Her brown eyes flashed with intelligence and I instantly liked her.

"John, it is so nice to meet you. I am Lillian," she said as she smiled.

Her hands were so delicate; I couldn't believe that she was a masseuse. "Ryan, would you please show John to the room. I will be there shortly."

He nodded and gestured for me to follow him. I watched her walk to a different room, her hips swaying back and forth and I couldn't help the twitch my cock gave at her sway.

The room that the butler led me to was large and dark. Candles were the only light in it and they covered various shelves and dressers. I could see hundreds of lotions on one table near the extra-large massage table that was resting in the middle of the room. Soft music played on the speakers in the wall and I felt a bit of my tension fade away.

In the corner was a curtain and Ryan motioned to it, "Please get completely undressed and wrap a towel around your waist. You will find one on the bench in there. When you are done, come out and get on the table."

I followed his directions, but as I slid my underwear off, I wondered if this was standard. I came out of the room and climbed up on the table. "Lie down on your stomach," he directed.

As I did, I felt him strap my legs and arms down onto the table. I tensed and asked, "Is this normal?"

"It is for Lillian."

Then I heard him leave the room. I lay there, wondering what was going on. I could hear another person enter the room and then her voice filled the room, "John, I am going to massage your entire body and all you have to do is relax. If you can relax enough, the massage will remove all the stress from your body."

I breathed in a deep gush of air and willed my body to relax. I felt her remove the towel from my waist and then I was completely exposed. Is this normal? I wondered again.

Hot liquid slid down my back and then her hands started kneading and massaging my back. I groaned at the pleasure that she was spreading through my muscles and she moved down my back slowly until she reached my hips. Then she rubbed her hands down my thighs and calves. Finally, her hands began rubbing my ass and I felt a twinge in my cock at how wonderful her hands felt.

The massaging seemed to last forever as she made her way back up to my back and down each of my legs again.

In a relaxed slumber, I could feel her cover me again and she said, "Turn over," as she undid the straps. I did as she told me. I jerked in surprise when I saw that she was completely naked. Her skin was golden and she looked like a goddess with her full breasts, narrow waist, and wide hips. Her long, brunette hair was down and it fell in waves around her shoulders. My cock jumped to attention and I tried to fight it, but she leaned over me, her breasts brushing my skin as she tied my hands and legs back down.

"I'm going to blindfold you for this part," she said and before I could say anything, a silky black blindfold covered my view of her.

I felt her hands slide along my body and the hot liquid soothed away the stress in my body as she worked my chest. I felt her lift off the covers and then her hands slid down my chest to my stomach. I shook under her, my cock growing harder with each passing second. The tension from work was changing to a different kind of tension as I tried to fight down my desire. I couldn't control my growing hardness, but if she didn't mind, then I didn't either.

Her hands slid down my legs, brushing my cock and I felt it weeping at her touch. I could imagine her naked body rubbing against mine, her full breasts pressing against me as she slides down my body.

I jerked under her touch as my body begged for release. Suddenly, I was pulled from my thoughts when she grabbed my cock and runs her nails over it. Her fist worked up and down my shaft and I groaned, my hips jutting forward. She palms the tip and rubs a circle over it; I shudder and bite back the need building up in me. As she rubs up and down my shaft, tremors shake through my body and I feel her other hand rub my balls. She slides one finger against the opening of my ass and I stiffen. She doesn't put it inside but she rubs the puckered flesh and I feel dizzy from the stimulation. I have never worked this hard not to explode.

As if reading my mind, she whispers, her breath tickling my cock, "Let go for me."

With those words, she began jacking my shaft up and down quickly and my cock exploded and I spewed my load all over her hand.   My orgasm shook my body and as I tried to gain control of my breathing, I felt her undoing my straps. As she laid the warm thick cover on me, she said, "Sleep now. I will return in one hour. Next time, you will not be strapped down." My cock jumped at the excitement and I felt my stress slowly wash away as I closed my eyes.

15 THE NURSE

Shuffling in my seat, I glance up at the large white clock on the wall. I hate medical offices and this one was no different. I was here for my physical exam and instead of visiting a physician, I was going to have my physical with the nurse practitioner. I glance around the waiting room, the white walls and gray chairs making it look dull, the only decoration a few plants, some magazines on the white coffee table, and the television quietly playing the news. It was like hundreds of other offices and I found it so boring that I attacked my emails as I waited.

"Mr. Emmett," the cool voice echoed and I looked up, my mouth dropping at how hot my nurse was. She had to be no more than thirty with honey blond hair and blue eyes. Her white nurse's uniform was crisp and clean and it clung to every curve of her body, including the ample breasts that were filling out the top.

I stood up and followed her into the small room with an exam table, desk and two chairs, including one used to draw blood samples. She turns to me and said in a husky voice, "Can you take off your shoes and step up on the scale in the hall?"

I nodded and moved over to the stand. I grinned at the weight as she clucked her teeth. I was trim and any weight

I had on me was pure muscle. I worked out daily and add that to the physical demands of my job and I was constantly exercising.

When we returned to the exam room, she pulled my history up on the computer sitting on the desk and browsed through it. "So, Mr. Emmett, why are you here today?"

"Call me Doug," I said with a wink and was rewarded with a pretty blush on her peaches and cream complexion, "I'm forty so I figure it is time for me to get a physical. Actually, it is mandatory for my job to make sure I can still handle the physical aspect of the job."

"Forty? I wouldn't put you past twenty five," she said and I could tell that she really was surprised.

As she stood up to grab the blood pressure cuff, I winked at her and said, "Well, I have the stamina of an eighteen year old."

Her blush deepened and she licked her lips quickly before she placed the cuff on my arm...or rather tried to place the cuff on my arm. "Oh my," she gasped, "Your bicep is so large, the cuff doesn't fit. I have to admit, I haven't seen a man in such great shape in a long time. How often do you work out?"

I beam with pride and can't help myself when I flex my bicep slightly, "Every day. If I am not working, I head to the gym for a good workout. My job is pretty physically demanding but it pays really well."

Her eyes sparkle and she gives a small laugh, "Well, I should go and get a different cuff so I can take your blood pressure," she said as she slipped out the door.

She was back before I could even look around the room and her hands shook as she slipped the cuff around my arm. Her fingers lingered on the skin and she bit her lip as she wrote down my numbers. "Can you get undressed and put on the robe; I will have to do a full exam, including a rectal exam."

As she explained the procedure, I groaned inwardly.

There was no way I could control myself with this beauty pawing at me, especially when she needed to check my prostate. Deciding to play with fire, I say, "Well, the only way you are getting my pants down is if you are bent over the exam table."

Her face went instantly red and I found myself grinning. I really liked how easily she reacted to me. Instead of replying, she moved to the cupboard and pulled out a dressing gown. She placed it on the table and grabbed the door knob. As she did I said, "So is that a yes?" She left without a reply.

Standing in the room, I eyed the dressing gown and considered running out of the room. The last thing I wanted was a rectal exam, but the thought of that sexy nurse running her hands over me was too much to pass up. Taking a deep breath, I strip completely and slide the gown on, my tight ass peeking through the thin fabric.

A short knock on the door made me look as she walked in and I almost groan at the sight of the stethoscope wrapped around her neck. I wonder if she realizes how sexy she is...and how naughty she would look.

"Okay, Mr. Emmett," she said as she motioned for me to sit on the exam table, "I am just going to check your vitals and make sure everything is okay with your heart and lungs. So you said you work out? Do you do cardio or just weight lifting?"

As she moved the stethoscope around on my chest, I felt a stirring in my groin. It was erotic as hell and I answered her questions as best as I could. Most of my energy was going towards not getting a hard-on while she was working. Even still, I could swear that her fingers were lingering too long on my body and she kept returning to my chest to check my heart. I groaned softly as the soft smell of her lavender perfume wafted to me, but she ignored me.

"Okay, I need to do a balance test, please stand up and walk heel to toe down the length of the room."

Walking back and forth, I ignored the fact that the gown had parted and she could see my ass. I could feel her eyes burning into my ass and I was sure that she was getting as hot as I was. I couldn't stop the erection that was throbbing against my thigh and I only hoped she couldn't see the outline of my stiff cock through the gown.

"Please remove your gown to your waist," her voice sighed and I turned to see her gazing at me, desire burning brightly in her eyes, "I need to look for anything unusual on the skin."

Slipping the gown down, my back to her, I jump slightly at the feel of her fingers on my skin. She runs them down the length of my back and then slides over my ass. I moan as my cock jumps to attention from the half erect state it has been in. She walks around me and her eyes widen at the sight of my large cock but she doesn't say anything. Instead, she runs her fingers over my stomach, making it clench as she touches a ticklish spot. I suck in my breath, but I stand there, proud as a statue that I look so good. She orders me to pull my gown back over my arms and to lift it from the bottom.

Her hand drops down to my groin and hovers over my cock. "I'm," she croaks before clearing her throat, "I have to check for hernias, please turn your head and cough."

As I do, she cups my balls and a jolt of electricity shoots through my cock right to the tip. My cough comes out as more of a groan but she doesn't move her hand away, instead, she strokes my balls and I close my eyes, breathing in slowly to keep from blowing my load onto her pretty hand. "I'm going to have to gather some blood work. Please pull your gown down and I will go and get the tray."

I look up at her surprised, "I don't do well with needles. Do you have anywhere for me to sit?"

She gestures to the chair used for blood work. As I sit down, she adjusts the seat so it is reclined and then she secures the straps on the chair around my arm. "If I didn't know better, I would think you were getting me all ready for something kinky," I wink at her.

She blushes, but leaves the room. My cock aches it is so hard and being tied up at her disposal makes it even harder. I think of all the usual gross and unattractive things trying to make my hard-on shrink.

When she comes back in, she is holding a tray with everything she needs for blood work. "If you want, close your eyes to relax. I will get this over with quickly."

I do as she says and close my eyes. I can hear her set the tray down but then I hear what sounds like a zipper. My eyes shoot open just as her dress falls to the ground. She steps out of it and moves in front of me. I groan at how perfect her breasts are, swaddled in a white lace bra. The matching lace thong is enough to have my cock leaking. She walks over to stand in front of me and leans down. Her lips are feather light on my ear and she says, "First, I need to test your endurance Mr. Emmett."

She places a kiss on my ear and slides her tongue inside. I shudder at the heat spreading through me as she moves to my neck and begins sucking and nipping it. She kisses along my jaw and then captures my mouth with a kiss. I let her take full control of the kiss, although I want to grab her and pull her against me. She nips at my mouth then slides her tongue into my mouth. I suck it deep and she moans against me, digging her hands into my short hair.

She crawls onto my lap and my cock slides against her thong. She groans into my mouth, her hips moving back and forth, my dick creating friction on her clit. As she shudders against me, she slides her thong to the side and then draws me into her hot slick wetness.

Dropping down on my cock, I am buried inside of her and she continues rocking back and forth. I can feel my orgasm building and I kiss her deeper, my teeth nipping at her mouth as we tongue fuck. My cock sliding in and out of her wetness as my tongue slides in and out of her mouth. She begins crying out, clenching against my cock and I explode, my climax forcing a cry from me that she swallows against her mouth. I come deep inside her and I can't believe how long I continue to writhe and unload in her before it finally stops.

She smiles down at me trying to catch her breath, "Well, I have to say you have passed your exam with flying colors...perfect penetration...great stamina. You can get dressed now." Confused that it was all over, I ask her about the rectal exam and the blood work. She laughs at me, comes close to my face and says hoarsely, "I've rescheduled your appointment with Dr. Martin. He'll make sure those penetrations are performed just as perfectly. "

16 THE MAID

Sitting in my home office going over the latest investment numbers, I glance up when I hear the alarm beep and a code being entered. I know who it is so I return to my work. I had reports to finish for several clients since I am their investment banker. I can hear Marcie moving around the house as she cleaned it.

Marcie had been my maid for three years. She was from Sweden, in the United States on a student visa, and she looked like she had just walked off the runway. Her straight blonde hair matched her pale complexion and pale, ice blue eyes. She was thin and tall, almost as tall as me, and she had small breasts that she rarely covered with a bra.

She came twice a week to clean my large home and I tried to be away when she did. The girl was a horrible flirt and one day I was going to take her flirting to the next level if she didn't stop. And I was pretty sure that was going to get me into trouble.

The last time I saw her, she had mentioned getting a uniform so she looked more professional. I had congratulated her on the idea and gone back to work; praying that her uniform was a little less revealing then her standard skin tight jeans.

Hearing her hand on my office door, I look up as she enters and my mouth drops. She isn't dressed in her usual jeans and t-shirt today. Instead, she is wearing black silk dress that ended at the top of her thighs. The square neckline of the dress shows off her cleavage and the white lace trim and apron, along with the white headband, are very sexy.

"You like my uniform?" She asks it in such an innocent voice that I try to hide the erection growing in my pants. This is no uniform; it is sexy French maid costume.

My mouth is dry and I try to swallow. "Yes, it is very nice," I croak.

She smiles and moves toward me but the phone rings. "Are you going to get that?" she asks, waving at the phone.

I pick up the handset, my hands shaking slightly as I bark, "Hello."

The voice on the other end is the client that has been extremely frustrating. She knew nothing about investments but she still wanted to have her hand in everything. I answer her questions as I watch Marcie dusting the book shelves. She leans down, her legs straight as she does and I can see her ass under the lace. I groan at the sight of her black, lace thong. "Sorry, nothing is wrong," I say to my client.

I continue talking about investments as Marcie makes her way around the room. She makes sure to bend low each time, giving me a view of either her ass or her breasts. As she comes around my desk, she leans over, looking like she is about to straddle me but instead, she gives me a teasing smile and bends over my desk, tidying the papers spread across it.

I reach out but stop myself from touching her. She turns around and captures my hand, sliding it up to her breast. I cup the small handful as she climbs up onto my lap. I lower the phone, but she shakes her head and places her finger on my lips. I put it back to my ear and continue to talk to my client as Marcie begins rocking her hips back and forth. I can feel her wet pussy through my slacks and my cock almost hurts from the pleasure she is giving me. I bite back the groan, trying to keep my voice even as I answer more questions for the annoying woman. I feel frustrated that my client won't shut up and frustrated that Marcie won't free my cock so I can plunge it into her.

She slides off of me and drops to her knees between my legs. Pulling my hips down, she opens my pants and pulls out my cock. She looks up at me and says, "You like?"

Before I can answer her, her mouth is wrapped around my cock, sliding it in until it is buried deep in her mouth . She sucks it deeper and I hear her gag slightly at my size. I jerk forward as she slides it back out, nipping it gently with her teeth as she does. I can't stop myself from moaning. She sucks the tip back in and grasps my shaft, each stroke pushing my dick into her wet mouth further.

She licks down the shaft and then sucks on my balls. I can see her rubbing her clit as she does and I come completely undone. I can't answer my client and instead, I start swearing, "Fuck yeah, suck my cock. Take it all."

Marcie obliges and she sucks me harder and faster, working her mouth and her hand as I groan and thrash under her. I cry out, "I'm going to come," as she nods her head.

Then I'm flooding her mouth and she swallows it up. I can hear her moaning as she gulps down mouthful after mouthful and I can't stop shooting it into her. She sucks me dry and I realize that I can hear my client screaming at me through the phone that she has never been so disgusted in her life. I laugh and hang up the phone, and then I gather my beautiful maid in my arms. "I *like* very much," I say before I strip her completely naked.

17 THE DELIVERY GUY

I stretch at my work desk and admire the custom earrings that I have created this morning. It is amazing how beautiful the emerald and diamond cluster sparkle in the gold setting and I feel pride about my work. I have been working from home, designing custom jewelry for three years and my work has definitely taken off. I have so many orders I can barely keep up.

The number of deliveries arriving and leaving my house has become a daily occurrence. Every morning, the delivery guy comes and drops off my latest supplies and every evening, another one comes to pick it up. It was getting so busy, I was constantly wondering if I should hire an assistant.

Rubbing the sore muscle at the back of my neck, I notice that my short red hair has grown a bit too long again. Keeping it in a short bob makes it so much easier to work without finding hair in my tools or in my eyes. Plus, I think the short hair really shows off my high cheekbones, clear green eyes and my full, red lips. It even looks amazing with the small dusting of freckles that cover my nose.

Needing a break from the work, I jump onto the

treadmill and run for a half hour, sweat breaking out at the nape of my neck and my heavy breasts sway with the movement. The workout is intense, I love running, despite my chest, and I am in amazing shape.

After the workout, I have a quick shower and change into a clingy, purple sundress, ignoring the bra today. I think about the delivery guy with his boy next door charm. His blond, sun kissed hair, his blue eyes and the dimple in his chin that I want to run my tongue over. He is taller than the last delivery guy, about six feet or so, and his shoulders are almost as wide as he is tall. You can definitely tell that he is a body builder with those hard pecks and thick legs. The man was definitely used to working his entire body.

The sound of the doorbell shakes me from my daydream and I check my appearance in the mirror before answering the door. I would be lying if I said it didn't matter but the reason why I was looking the way I did today was because I knew when he was going to come.

He was fairly new, only been running my deliveries for the last week. He always called me ma'am, always made sure my deliveries were on time, even making extra deliveries if he needed to during the day. I found that as interesting as his body. He seemed to know that I ran my business by the clock.

As I swung open the door, I smiled in victory as his eyes slid from the toe ring on my bare feet up my smooth legs until they hovered at my breasts. I could see my nipples jutting through the silk fabric and how he licked his lips. His eyes filled with desire and I could see his thick package bulging against the seam of his pants. My clit shuddered at the reaction he was having for me, but instead of cupping his shaft, I took the clipboard from him and signed for my package.

"Have a nice day, ma'am," he drawled and I almost curled my toes in response.

I closed the door behind him and leaned against it,

"You dummy, invite him in next time."

Returning to my desk, I sat down and tackled the necklace that I was doing for a rich socialite in New York. She was a regular client, but she hated to wait so I always bumped other work for hers.

A few hours later, I glanced up at the clock and realized that I had worked through most of the day. Four o'clock flashed on the display just as the doorbell rang.

Getting up, I opened the door to find the delivery guy again, holding another package for me. His gaze raked over me again and I couldn't help but notice that his cock was hard again. "Sorry, ma'am, but this package got overlooked when I delivered the last one," he said apologetically.

I took the package as he said, "There's a duty fee for this one so I will need a check for the amount."

"Oh, my check book is in my office. Why don't you come in and set the package down on the desk," I say as excitement runs through me.

He follows me through the house to my workspace and as I am writing the check, he looks around. "That's a beautiful necklace ma'am."

"Thanks," I beam with pride, "It is for a client in New York; I am going to be done with it soon and will need to send it out on a late delivery."

He turns to me and takes a step forward, "You look good in glasses, do you wear them often?"

I touch the glasses, realizing that I had forgotten to take them off, "No, just when I am working on an intricate design."

"Well, if you don't mind me saying, you look hot in them," he says and I gasp at the need that races through me. I want him to stop flirting and take action.

Hesitating as I hand him the check, he looks towards the package. "I guess I should get going? Is there anything else that you needed today?"

I glance at the package and say, "You know, I was

expecting one more package, are you sure it is not in your truck," he shakes his head, "Or maybe at the depot," I add quickly.

"Not sure, but I can check and deliver it if it is," he says.

I sigh in mock relief, "That would be wonderful. Do you mind driving out here again if it is? It really is an important piece."

"Not at all," he smiles and I follow him back to the door.

I close the door, overjoyed that I would get to see him again. Returning back to work, I find that I can't concentrate as the hours slip by. The necklace is almost finished when I finally give up and make myself a light dinner. I glance at the clock, jumping at every car that passes, but my delivery guy still hasn't shown up.

At nine, I finally realize that he isn't coming and head to the shower so I can ease the ache that has been sitting in my clit all day. The steam in the shower is just building up when I hear the doorbell.

Wrapping my short robe around me, I walk to the door and open it. Standing on the other side is my delivery guy. He grins sheepishly at me, his hands empty as he says, "There was no package for you at the depot. I wasn't going to bother you, but I was worried that you needed it to finish up the necklace. I thought I would let you know that it wasn't in yet so you didn't worry."

My mouth drops at the surprise and I know that he wants me as badly as I want him. Why else would he come all this way? "Oh, I did need it but it isn't your fault," I say, fake frustration filling my voice, "Why don't you come in for a drink...so I can thank you for taking the time to come and tell me."

I open the door wide and smile wider as he accepts my invitation and walks in. I grab him a cold beer from the fridge and hand it to him, taking one for myself.

I sit down at the kitchen island and allow my robe to

slip slightly to show off my ample bosom. His eyes darken as he takes a long swallow of his beer. Sitting down beside me, he says, "Is your husband home?"

"I don't have a husband...or a boyfriend."

I slide my foot up his leg and then back down, my fingers playing with the belt of my robe. I take a small sip of my beer and continue to watch him as my foot slides between his legs. I gently massage the bulge in his pants and bite my lip playfully.

"You sure?" he asks me, his voice a rumble in his chest.

"Oh, very sure," I say and then I remove my robe, showing him just how sure I am.

He reaches for me and I playfully pull back, standing up. He rises to give chase, but I move into him, pressing my body against him. I take my beer and pour a small amount onto my chest, laughing as the cold liquid teases my skin.

Then his mouth is on me, lapping up the beer and sucking it off. Each suck of my nipple that he takes makes me feel like he is sucking my clit. I run my hands over his chest and drop down to his bulge.

Manoeuvring his pants open, I free his cock. Bending down, I take his shaft into my mouth and begin sucking it. I can feel his hands sliding down my back and he cups my ass, pulling me closer to him. I tip my beer onto the tip of his cock and begin lapping up the liquid. I can taste his saltiness with the beer and I groan at the heady taste.

His hands slide along the crack of my ass and I can feel him playing with the tight pucker of the entrance. I groan as I feel his finger penetrate the opening of my ass and I stop sucking for a moment, not sure if I want to keep going – then his other finger slides into my pussy and I can't stop shaking from how good it feels.

Swallowing him with a renewed urgency, his finger starts swirling over my clit as another finger fill me. I rock back and forth, timing my movements with his fingers, his cock glides in and out of my mouth and he fists the back of my head with his other hand, urging himself deeper into my mouth. His body starts to shake and I can feel my own orgasm building as his fingers fuck my ass and pussy. I scream out my orgasm around his cock as he cries out, "I'm going to come."

He tries to pull me off, but I swallow him deeper and his load shoots down my throat. I swallow the hot load, licking him clean before I stand up.

I smile at him and laugh as I notice that his cock is growing hard again. "Already?"

He rips his shirt from his body and kicks his pants free and then he is standing there in all his naked glory.

Lifting me up, he sets me on the island and I wrap my legs around his waist. I can feel his hard shaft pressing into my clit and I wiggle around on it, encouraging him to enter me. He thrusts into me at the exact moment that his tongue plunges into my mouth.

His movements are fast and hard and his tongue twines with me as he swallows my moans. I can feel my second orgasm building, threatening to send me over the edge as he rhythmically pounds in and out of me. As I start to thrash from the flood of pleasure ripping through me, I hear him cry out as he comes for a second time. My pussy tightens around his shaft as I orgasm again and then we both collapse onto each other panting.

I smile as I feel his cock growing hard inside me again and I say, "Let's head to the bedroom and you can give me my third delivery."

18 THE POLICE OFFICER

The party at the Phi Beta C house was in full swing when I finally showed up. I hadn't planned on going but I had passed my Bio-Chem final and this was the reward that I needed. I navigated the busy dorm house but the crowd was enormous. It was definitely the biggest party of the year.

I felt a hand slide across my ass and I jumped, glancing around to see who had done it, but I couldn't find anyone. Instead, I found my roommate in the corner making out with her boyfriend. I tried to get her attention, but it wasn't until I was almost beside her that she noticed me. Jumping up, Melissa gave me a firm hug and said, "I'm so glad you made it Anna. I didn't think you were going to come."

Irritation flashed through me. I hated crowds and tonight was supposed to be a girl's night. Why was she busy making out with her boyfriend when she was supposed to be hanging out with me? As though she had read my thoughts, she said, "Why don't we go upstairs and find a place to just hang out?"

I nod and she slid her hand in mine while taking her boyfriend's hand in her other hand. Following her up the stairs, I blush as she bursts through a door. Inside is two girls and a guy and they are groping and kissing each other. The guy is perched behind a brunette, his cock buried deep inside her as the brunette is busy licking the slit of another brunette. I feel desire burn through me but Melissa giggles and says, "Oh, sorry to bother you."

She closes the door and moves down the hallway. Carefully checking the next room, she pulls me into the room and onto a bed. Laughing, she says, "Why don't we just hang out? Please don't leave, Anna."

I sigh and sit on the bed beside her, feeling uncomfortable as her boyfriend leans down and kisses her. He pushes her down on the bed and grabs her breast, massaging it as he continues to kiss her. She spreads her legs and allows him to nestle between them. He rocks his hips, dry humping her. I groan in frustration, and he looks back at me.

Melissa grins, "I think Anna is jealous."

"Well, we can always recreate that threesome we just saw," he says, desire filling his eyes as he looks at my breasts.

"Screw you," I say to both of them before I jump off the bed and storm out of the room. My anger takes me down the stairs and out of the party and I am half way home before I realize where I had planned on going.

I hear the horn of a car behind me and I turn around to see a police cruiser. The officer pulls up alongside of me. "Excuse me. Are you coming from the party at the Phi Beta C house?"

I nod, "I haven't been drinking officer. My night was ruined shortly after I got there when my friend's boyfriend asked me to join them in a threesome."

I blush at how forward I am being. I turn away and hear him getting out of the car. As I turn around, my mouth drops. There is the most gorgeous man I have ever seen. He looks like a stripper with the uniform straining on his muscles. I can see a large bulge in his groin area and I get wet instantly. He has sandy blonde hair and gray eyes and I practically melt under his gaze.

"Wow, sounds like tonight was not your night."

"I know right. The guy is a complete sleaze. If I was going to have a threesome, it wouldn't be with him."

He clears his throat and I gaze up at him. He looks unsure of what to do and all I want to do is wrap my arms around him. "Look, you shouldn't be walking at night alone," he says, "Do you have someone you can call to have meet you?"

I shake my head, "Everyone I know is at the party."

I hesitate and glance around, "Look, could you give me a ride? I'm not that far. Besides, isn't your job to protect and serve?"

He glances down the street, looking at the dark paths I would have to take. "You are in luck," he finally says, "I just got off right before I stopped you."

He motions to the car and I move around to the passenger seat. I hike up my mini skirt so I can flash him a small amount of my panties. I smile when I see him swallow. He definitely noticed.

"So where am I taking you?"

"The old dorms behind Center Hall."

He pulls away from the curb and I lean back into the seat, spreading my legs wide as I do. I can see his eyes returning to my long legs time and time again as I chat with him about my major. Finally, I say, "Are you single?"

"Umm, yeah, I'm single."

"And do you like girls," I tease.

He scowls at me, "Yes, I like girls. Why would you think otherwise?"

"Because you have barely looked at my panties," I feel brazen with how I am talking to him, but I can't help it.

As he pulls up to my building, I ask, "Can you drop me off in the underground parking? I can take the elevator from there."

He nods and navigates the car into the parking lot. It is

empty, just like I knew it would be. When he parks the car, I get out and move to the back of the car. He does the same, his eyes never leaving me. I lean over the side of the trunk, facing him. "You know, I have always had a fantasy about a police officer," I say, licking my lips and spreading my hands along the trunk.

"Yeah, and what would that fantasy be," he asks, leaning towards me.

Standing up, I walk to the back of the trunk and place my hands flat on the top of it. I spread my legs wide and lean forward. "That I have been a very naughty girl and a police officer has to come up behind me and search me."

He moves around behind me and I can feel him standing there, heat coming off of him. He slides his leg between mine and presses up on my slit. I groan at the desire pulsing through me and spread my legs a little wider. His hands come around and he cups my breasts, rubbing his thumb over my nipple. I arch against him and I can feel his hard bulge against my ass. I rock against him, letting him dry hump me as I do.

His hands slide down my body and he cups my ass before he slides his fingers under my skirt. He runs them up my slit and then starts to rub my clit. I squirm under him and the moan that comes out of me is full of desire. I can barely talk when I say, "I have been such a bad girl, and I need to be cuffed."

He growls and bites the back of my neck before he roughly grabs my hands. He pulls my arms behind my back and cuffs me. Pushing me forward onto the trunk, he rubs his hard shaft against my ass. I groan, "I need to be punished. I need this punishment for being so bad."

His hand slips under my skirt again and I murmur, "Fuck yeah, just like that," as his hands slide along my folds. He twists my underwear and rips them off.

I can feel my body dripping; I am so wet for him and he feels it too with his fingers. I can feel him undoing his pants and then he is thrusting inside of me pushing me forward onto the trunk. I cry out in pleasure and rock back to him as he thrusts into me again and again. The intensity grows without the use of my hands as he holds onto the cuffs, pulling me against his thick cock as it slides deep into me over and over again.

He moves harder and faster and I can feel tears in my eyes from how good it feels. I begin to scream in passion as I hear him roar and then we are both coming together, riding our orgasms to the greatest heights. I can feel his cock pulsing deep within me as I shake and spasm around his hardness. I feel him un-cuff my hands as the last shudder of glory ripples through me.

Recovering he kisses my shoulder and I say, "My legs are wobbly, I think you should walk me to my room now. I need additional protection and servicing."

He laughs with desire flaring in his eyes again and says, "Lead the way."

19 THE FIREMAN

The shrill scream of the alarm jerked me from my book and I watched as the firehouse sprang to life. I have lived across from it for 6 years and I knew that that activity meant...there was a fire. Clicking on my radio, I listened in on the call...large house fire in progress.

I grimaced as the men I knew well rushed to the scene. I had cooked for them over the years and every time they went out, I worried about them all from the Captain on down to the new rookie that just started a week ago. I didn't know him at all but I did know he was extremely good looking with his short cut auburn hair, brown eyes and crooked grin. He stood six foot two and had a build that should be featured in a firemen calendar.

I didn't notice the other firemen. Most were married, but not this one. As a single, red blooded American girl, I couldn't help but look and dream that maybe I would get to ride that fireman's hose.

Shaking myself from my daydream, I watch the clock. Several hours later, a tired looking fire engine pulls back into the station and I wave at the captain. Crossing the street, I hear him call out, "All safe," before he turns to his men, "Good work guys. Now let's get cleaned up and wash the truck up."

I return to my yard to do some weeding, but I notice the rookie coming out of the firehouse. His chest is bare and the tanned skin glistens with his sweat. My mouth goes dry and I try to avoid looking at him, but I can't help it. I watch him scrub the fire truck and lose myself fantasizing about him running those firm hands over me. I would be standing in the shower, water flowing down my firm breasts as he rubs soap along the nipple. His chiseled body pressed into me and his hardness sliding up my slippery crack.

Seeing him wave at me, I blush, wave back quickly, and duck into my house. I can't believe he caught me staring. Instead of staring out the window at him, I focus my attention on making dinner. As I am cooking, I decide to bake a cake for the guys to thank them for their work.

When it is nearly finished, I hear a short knock on the door. I jump and glance outside at the dark street. The knock comes again and I slowly open the door. Standing in the light of my kitchen is the very tall and very sexy rookie, in his full uniform, hat and all.

I gaze up at him, my nipples hardening as he takes in my dress. My long legs are bare except for a pair of short spandex shorts and my tight stomach is visible under the braless tank top I am wearing. My blond hair falls around my shoulders and I know my blue eyes are blazing. I want him.

"Yes?" I breathe the question with a husky voice.

He opens his mouth and a small croak comes out. Clearing his throat, he tries again, "Ma'am, the Captain sent me over here to see if you had any garlic salt."

I raise my eyebrow in question and he quickly answers, "It's spaghetti night."

Nodding my head, I open the door wide in invitation. As he enters, I look over his attire and ask, "Why are you in full gear? Alec isn't it?"

A blush creeps into his cheeks and I fight the urge to cup his face in my hand. It is sweet that he is so bashful, I think to myself. "Yeah. It's the guys. I am still going through a bit of hazing. After tonight, I'll be done," he says.

"Well, you must be boiling. You can take off your jacket while I find the garlic salt."

Blushing even deeper, he shakes his head, "I would love to ma'am, but I'm not wearing anything underneath."

Now it's my time to blush as wicked thoughts race through my head. My gaze drops to his stomach before I turn back to him and give him a wink, "Nothing I haven't seen before...after all, I was watching you clean the truck today."

Turning back to the cupboard, I grab the garlic salt and hand it to him, hesitating, "You know I was just finishing a cake for you guys. If you don't mind waiting ten minutes, you could take it with you."

He glances out the window towards the firehouse and nods, "Sure, sounds good."

Stripping off his jacket, my eyes widen at the sight of his muscular chest. I long to touch it and I can't help it when my eyes follow the line of light hair down his chest to his navel. From the v peeking out from his pants, he isn't wearing anything under them either. I sigh longingly as I turn back to the counter. One flick of my finger to his suspenders I could have him completely bared.

Clearing the lust from my throat I ask, "So how long have you been a fireman?"

"About a year now. I was at my dad's station house up until last week, but I really wanted to get out on my own."

"Oh, your dad's a fireman?" The small talk is keeping me from ripping his clothes off as I pour the ingredients for the strawberry icing into the bowl.

I see him out of the corner of my eye come up beside me and lean against the counter. My hands shake as I lift the electric mixer up and into the bowl. "Yeah, my dad and my two brothers are firemen. My sister is a nurse, along with my mom," he shrugs, "I guess it is a family business."

He leans in towards me and I punch the button of the mixer. The blades shoot out, spraying strawberry icing everywhere – on the counter, the window, my top and across Alec's chest. "Oh my god! I am so sorry Alec," I shout as I flip the switch off the mixer.

He laughs, "Don't worry about it," as I reach for the towel.

Wetting it down, I return to Alec and rub a small amount of the icing off. Gazing into his eyes, I gather my courage and quickly swipe his strawberry covered nipple with my tongue. I close my eyes in pleasure and make a soft moan. He tastes amazing.

Before he can push me away, I tiptoe up and I kiss him deeply, nipping at his mouth as I suck in his lower lip. He groans and wraps his arms around me. I can feel his hard member pressing into my stomach and I sigh into him.

My mouth opens as his tongue licks inside it and I feel my knees go weak. Only he was holding me up and keeping me from sliding to the kitchen floor. He releases me long enough to move to my neck and I push him away from me until he is pressed against the table where I begin licking up and down his chest. I push the suspenders off of his chest and allow his pants to slide down to the floor. He is hard and ready and I grin up at him.

He reaches down and pulls my shirt up and off of my body. He leans down and sucks my breast into his mouth and licks off the strawberry smeared on my stomach. I groan at the sensations running through me as he chuckles into my skin. "The icing is delicious," he says wickedly and returns to licking and sucking my nipple.

I thread my hands in his hair and hold him to my nipple. The frustration I have been feeling for a week continues to grow in me as he teases and tortures my flesh. I feel my clit throbbing with need and I slide the shorts down my body. He groans as he realizes I am not wearing any underwear and his hand shoots between my legs, sliding up and down the silky folds of my hot center.

I grind against his hand, begging him to slide a finger into me before I growl in frustration. Pushing his back onto the table, I jump to straddle him. Before I can finish licking the rest of the icing from his chest I hear a snap and we fall to the floor surrounded by the broken table. Laughing hysterically, Alec rolls us out of the debris into the foyer before I can withdraw in embarrassment. Not ruining the moment, he cupped my face, leaned down and kissed me softly. I roll him back over and climb back on top. I make my way down to his shaft looking up at him with gratitude dancing in my eyes. I take him into my mouth and I bite him playfully. I hear him suck in his breath at my assault. I glance up at him as my tongue soothes the sore flesh before I graze his shaft with my teeth again. He moans and juts his hips out to me.

I work my teeth up and down his hardness, biting, licking and soothing his flesh as I do before I swallow him entirely. I can feel it stretching my throat as it slides down and I swallow around it, loving the way it jumps in my mouth as I do.

My frustration comes boiling to the surface and I suck harder, taking more of him in. I slip my hands between my legs and press on my throbbing clit before sliding a finger into my pussy. I start moving to a rhythm – taking him deep inside my mouth as my finger pushes deep inside me before I slide him out. I can hear him grunting in time, his fists banging on the floor as he fights for control.

It doesn't work and my last hard suck is enough for him to lose control and he pushes me off of him. I roll over, my ass up in the air. He presses against my back with his hands as he positions his cock at my wet entrance, then he thrusts into me, driving me hard against the floor.

"Oh yes, Alec. Take me like that...I need you to fuck me harder."

He roars in excitement and begins pounding into me. I scream against him, urging him on as the sound of his cock slapping into me fills the room. He slaps my ass hard and tells me to come for him. He orders me to play with my clit as he drives harder and faster. I start screaming his name as he slides his hard shaft out, pumps it forcefully back in twice and then we are both crying out as ecstasy washes over us.

As our breathing begins to slow, he moves us onto our sides, still inside me. My smoke alarm goes off screaming us to action. I hear Alec laugh and say, "I think your cake is burning."

I turn to him and say, "It's a good thing I know a fireman."

20 THE GUY FROM THE GYM

I was mentally worn out from the day's stresses at work when I approached the doors that lead into my gym. I checked myself, knowing I was in such a bad mood, I probably should have headed straight home. A lot of good the gym was going to do me after a day like I had.

I paid for a bottle of water and scanned my key card. When I barged through the swinging doors, I hit what felt like a brick wall and fell to the floor with my contents flying around me. My first instinct was to cuss out the jerk that was standing in the way, until I looked up and saw a pair of stunning blue eyes. They were so light and so blue; I had never seen anything quite like them. I tried to scan the rest of his body as I gathered my things, but with my split attention, I kept fumbling everything.

He apologized profusely and he might have said something else, but I couldn't get my mind or my body to stay focused enough to be polite. He smiled a million dollar smile and walked off after he helped me gather all my things.

My God this man was fine! I caught myself staring; mouth agape, as I watched him straddle the first machine. I tripped on my way to put my things away and almost fell again.

I took a deep breath, put away my gym bag and car keys and walked all the way to the other side of the gym where the treadmills where located. Out of sight, out of mind right? Not when he decides to move over to the free weights in my area. I turned up my music and began my workout. I ran harder, picking up the pace, but it provided no distraction from this man. He was gorgeous. I never realized before that muscle definition like that existed. His arms and shoulders where large and strong and so very well defined. I was a tiny bit shocked to find myself getting a little wet in the middle of my run. The thud of my feet hitting the treadmill with each stride did nothing but make me feel even hotter, the rhythm mimicking wickedly delicious and fast-paced fucking.

What am I thinking?!

He caught me watching him several times and because I was looking at his body instead of his eyes, I couldn't be sure how long he watched me stare at him each time. At this point, I didn't care. He was magnificent. When he pulled the bottom of his shirt up to wipe away his sweat, I got a glimpse of that flat deep V of his abs that just begged to be licked.

When he was finally drenched in his own sweat and proceeded to take his shirt off completely, I almost came. I let out a grunt of frustration as I tried to keep it together on the treadmill. His stomach muscles were so defined and chiseled and his chest was broad and tight, like the statue of a Greek god.

I couldn't take it anymore. I knew I wouldn't be able to get in a good workout as long as he was near. I hit stop on my treadmill when I finished my fifth mile and took myself to the showers. My frustration was even worse. I was stressed out when I arrived and now my body was begging for a release I knew I couldn't give myself here in the gym.

I stripped naked and headed into the private shower hoping the cold water would ease some of my tension. I washed my hair and began soaping my body when I heard something behind me.

"Here, let me do that for you." Taken completely by surprise, I stood still, in shock. I had a gorgeous, strong, and virile man behind me and my body was soaking wet – and not from the water. "I saw you watching me," he said. All I could do was nod, wondering how he had gotten into the showers without being seen and not caring at the same time.

Still facing the wall, he took the soap from my hands and from behind to begin washing my breasts. My nipples were hard from excitement and pleasure. He drifted lower, washing my stomach, and then his hands returned to my breasts. He washed them over and over again and I don't know if it was watching the soap slide down my body or the growing steam from the shower, but my body weakened. I leaned my weight into him.

He washed my back slowly, kissing my neck softly. I tried to reach around for him and he grabbed my wrist to stop me.

"No. Not yet," he whispered. He dropped the soap, rinsed his hand, and began that short journey to the junction between my thighs as the other hand continued to play with my right breast, pinching my nipple and flicking the end of it quickly with the pad of his finger. As soon as his other hand reached my clit, I moaned in pure pleasure. I arched my back into him and that's when I could feel all of him. His cock stood up straight against his belly, pressed between us as he started to finger me. He was slick and wet and rubbing against me and my body was begging for release.

My breathing grew ragged and he could tell I was close. He turned me around to face him, penetrating me with those intense blue eyes. Without taking his eyes from mine, he deftly lifted me up and put my back against the wall. In one quick motion he entered me and drove in deep, burying himself completely inside me.

He waited a minute for me to acclimate to his size and then he drove into me again. His strong arms supported me and his large hands held onto my ass as he slowly drilled his throbbing cock to the hilt with each thrust. The tingling sensation began to build up again and I knew I was about to be done.

Thrust after thrust he entered me and since my back was against the shower it helped brace the movement, allowing me to feel all of him each time he entered me. He slowed down just enough to push me to the edge. When he knew I was there, he thrust into me harder and faster until I came so hard, dripping around his engorged manhood. I let out a long bellowing scream, releasing all the tension in my body as I felt him jerk, growl and come hard inside me. He continued to thrust slowly, draining every drop into me. His eyes were still open and focused on mine when I finally opened mine, smiling serenely.

I leaned back against the shower wall and whispered, "Now, *that* was a good workout."

21 THE PERSONAL TRAINER

The Crossfit class was really busy tonight and I had no doubt that the crowded room had more to do with the hot instructor than the actual program. The fact that he looked like he just jumped out of the cover of a male fitness magazine was not overlooked by the thirty women in the room.

I sighed as he ran us through a few exercise. I was head over heels for this guy. He had a wide chest and his six pack was so hard you could probably cut diamonds on it. His ass was tight and perfect and he had the largest biceps I had ever seen. He had a chiselled jaw and short military cropped hair.

Since I had started his class, I had transformed from an average Jane into a hard body. My breasts were perky and tight, my abs beautifully sculpted and my arms and legs shapely, but all still very feminine. I loved the way I looked with my long blonde hair and I had decided to add in some dark streaks. It matched my tanned complexion and blue eyes perfectly. I was positive that my instructor approved of my new look, if the way he watched me was any indication.

As we worked out today, he watched me and said to the class, "Do you see Angela? She is still having some issues with the Olympic lifts. She is going to hurt herself if she doesn't learn to correct her lifts."

I grin at the perfect opportunity and say, "Well, can I hire you as a personal trainer to learn the correct way?"

His eyes glow with approval and he nods. "It will have to be after hours, which is the only time I have available."

My pulse leaps at the hours I get to spend with him, all alone, just the two of us. As the class comes to an end, he draws me to the side and says, "Be here at eight tonight and I will run you through the areas you need to improve on."

I shudder at the promise in his words and head home to get ready.

****

At eight o'clock, I stand in front of the gym in my best work out clothes. The half top barely covers my entire breasts and the spandex shorts are so tight and short that you can see a panty line perfectly...that is if I was wearing panties. I knock on the glass door and see him look up from the front desk. He grins but then his eyes fill with desire as he takes in my appearance.

He lets me in and leads me back to the area where we stretch. He runs me through a quick warm-up and I feel hotter than ever when I am done. His gaze follows my movements as I stretch and I can't help but feel his gaze deep in my body. I feel a coil of need building inside of me, but I shake it off when he says, "We need to look at how you do your squats with the bar."

He places the bar on my shoulder and has me do a squat. His sigh is loud as he says, "You aren't going low enough and you keep coming up on your toes."

I try to correct my stance but again, he sighs. "Do you mind if I touch you?" I shake my head, my mouth going dry as I think about his large hands on me. He takes the bar from me and sets it down.

Then they are on me, grasping my waist as he stands behind me. He guides me into a squat, his hands slide down to my ass as I go down and he moans softly in my ear. He moves around in front of me and pulls my knees slightly apart. I lose my balance and fall backwards.

I gaze up at him as I laugh. He squats down and asks, "Are you okay?"

I nod, "Yes, just embarrassed," I say, then my laughter dies and I am staring up into his eyes. He leans forward and desire buffets me. I want to pull him down on top of me and he looks like he wants to lay on me. I clear my throat, trying to find my voice.

He extends his hand and when I take it, he pulls me up and we start again. He tries to get me to squat without buckling my knees and he even slid a box between my legs. I had wanted something else slid between my legs but it did help me do my squats.

During the entire hour, his hands are on me, correcting my posture but while his touch didn't feel too intimate, it burned my skin and I was panting, not from the squats but from his touch. Finally, filled with frustration, I put down the bar and head out the backdoor without saying anything to him.

Breathing in the cold air, I feel a little more under control. My clit still throbbed with need, but I could at least feel like there was some semblance of me. He comes out of the gym as I take in another large swallow of air and his musky scent fills my nostrils, causing that ache through me again. He touches my hand and then passes me some water. I take a deep swallow and watch him follow the movement of my breast.

I yearn for him to cup my breasts and cool the heat that is spreading through them. I work out the kink in my shoulders and he says, "Don't worry, you'll get it. You just have to keep your knees apart."

I laugh, choking on the water and he chuckles. The sexual undertones are clear between us and I know that he wants me as much as I want him. I turn to him and without hesitating I wrap my arms around him and kiss him. I don't make the kiss gentle, but put all my sexual frustration into it. He returns the kiss, just as hungry as my own. I wrap my legs around his waist and he lifts me up, grabbing my ass. He carries me into the gym and lays me down on the mats.

I lift my tank top off of my body and expose my bare breasts to him. He licks down my skin until he has my breast in his mouth and he sucks deeply. I buck against him, aching for him to enter me. His hands slide down my body and he pulls my shorts off. I lay on the mat, completely exposed to him, my body shaved and waiting for him.

He presses my legs open and rubs his thumb over my clit. My body feels like it is humming in anticipation. He breathes in my scent, then his tongue licks up my slit and I almost jump off of the mat. He chuckles and holds me down, lapping at my clit. I moan thrashing my head back and forth as he sucks on my clit. His finger slides into my wet depths and I shudder around him.

I am on fire when he finally lifts up and slides his own shorts and shirt off. I draw in my breath at the beauty of this man. He slides between my legs, his cock pressing against my entrance. He slowly pushes inside of me and I wrap my legs around him, urging him deeper.

He groans as he thrusts deep inside me. He kisses me deeply, his teeth clashing with mine as he thrusts in and out. I cling to him, my nails raking his back as I fight for the orgasm that is hovering right out of reach. Then he thrusts faster and harder into me and I come undone, crying out his name as he grunts through his climax. I can feel his load spilling deep inside me then he leans down and whispers, "Your form was perfect."

22 THE COWORKER

It wasn't like this was the first time I had seen him but today, there was something about him that was making my panties wet – well, more than usual. That he was hot was not disputed by anyone. All the girls in the office drooled over him. He was from the Italian office, just transferred to our North American office to make it more efficient.

His accent was heavy, but his English was flawless, as flawless as his olive complexion, dark, almost black eyes and black hair. Late at night, his smooth cheeks would be covered in a thick five o'clock shadow that made the girls melt like chocolate. I had fallen for him the moment he had walked into the office in his tailored suit. He was tall, about six foot three and he towered over my five foot five frame.

The first time I saw him out of the office was when he had walked into the boot camp class I take. Three times a week, I would watch his trim physique as he went through the gruelling workout and it left me panting and aching – and not because of the work out.

Still, I kept my distance; acted like I was indifferent, but he wasn't like any of the other men in the company. I rarely saw him at work since he was in a different department and he didn't seem to notice my cool demeanor, even though a fire of need raged underneath my dusty skin. I would exchange pleasantries, say hello but we never flirted. Flirting was saved for the other girls in the office.

Maybe that was why I was sitting here today. My panties wet, my clit throbbing with need as I gazed longing at him with my amber colored eyes. I played with my dark curls and sucked the tip of my pen as I watched his presentation. His eyes kept flicking back to me, but he seemed eager to leave. As the presentation ended, the girls flocked around him, running the occasional hand up his arm, flirting.

Feeling slight agitation, I left and headed back to my office. I had a full weekend of work to get caught up on, the annual audit sitting on my desk to finish. I finish for the night and return Saturday morning to tackle the rest of the work.

Around noon, I stretched at my desk and hit print on the file I was working on. Growling in frustration that my ink was empty, I head over to the supply room to grab more ink. Finding the ink, I turn back to the door, grasp the handle and find that it is locked. "Oh my god!" I shout to myself. The room is filled with shelving units and office supplies and as I glance around the room, I realize that there are no phones. I check the pockets of my slacks and remember that my own phone is sitting on my desk.

Banging on the door, I yell, "Hello! Can anyone hear me? Please, I am stuck in the supply closet."

The heavy wooden door rocks on its hinges under my fist but no one comes to open the door. After an hour of banging, I give up and slump into a discarded chair that is in the corner. Tears sting my eyes I wonder how long it will take for someone to find me. As I sit and wait, my eyes slide close and I feel myself drifting off to sleep.

"What are you doing in here? Are you okay?"

The thick, Italian accent, along with a light slap on my cheeks, jerks me awake and I jump up screaming. Rafael jumps back as I swing and captures my hand in his large hand. I stare at the object of my affection, desire burning through me at the sight of his chocolate eyes before I remember...the door!

Racing towards it, I find that it is still closed and locked tight. "No! The door is locked and we can't get out," I groan as I turn towards him.

He is standing beside a shelving unit, his hands shoved into a pair of jeans and a tight, t-shirt stretched across his chest with a guilty look on his face. His normally pristine hair is tousled and I long to run my hands through it. Shaking my head, I think to myself, now is not the time Jenny. "Do you have a key for the door," I ask hesitantly.

He spreads out his hand and shakes his head. "Sorry, no."

I sigh and slump down onto the floor. "Then it looks like we are stuck here."

He grins, much too happy in my mind, and sits down beside me. "That is okay, we can spend the time talking," he says cheerfully.

I spear him with a dirty look, but the opportunity to chat is better than nothing. I smile and say, "How do you like the US?"

His eyes bore into me before he says, "It is nice - everyone is so friendly."

And with those words, he launches into his life. I find myself enjoying the time with him as we talk about our family and our home towns. He talks of the hills of Italy and the vineyard his family owns – which is the best wine around here, he tells me. I talk about my job and we laugh as we try to find ways to escape. He even tried hoisting me up into the ceiling tiles at one point. It didn't work, but I did find myself falling into his strong arms laughing.

Finally defeated, we lay down on the floor as he props himself up on one arm. His gaze turns serious as he says, "Why don't you like me Jenny? All the other girls have asked me out, but not you."

I laugh away my discomfort before saying, "I don't

dislike you. It's just that...I never asked you out because all the other girls did."

I blush at the longing in my voice and watch as he slowly leans toward me. His lips are feather soft on mine as he kisses me. He raises his head and I can see desire burning in his chocolate eyes. His gaze searches my face looking for resistance and I lay still, worried that I will break this spell he is building in me. I can't fight the heat flowing through me or the way my panties have become wet at his scent.

He leans back down and his lips press into mine again, only harder this time. His mouth opens and I feel his tongue flick across my lips as his thumb runs along my jaw. I open up to him and his tongue invades my mouth, licking against my teeth. I feel him suck my lower lip into his mouth and he rakes his teeth against it. I groan in pleasure and he deepens his kiss even more as he lies on top of me. I can feel his hard shaft digging into my hip and my eyes widen at how ready he is.

I wrap my arms around him and tilt my head as he drags kisses down my jaw and onto my neck. I slide my hands under his shirt and drag my nails up his back. I break contact with him for just a moment as I pull his shirt over his head and down his arms. His chest is magnificent and covered with dark hair that tapers down into his jeans. I can't help but follow that line and he nips at my neck to bring my focus back to his eyes.

I see the need in them and with shaking hands, I unbutton my shirt and let it fall open then I unclasp the front of my bra, it too falling open revealing my breasts. He cups my breasts and I smile at how perfectly they fit in his hands before I close my eyes in ecstasy. He flicks my hard, rose colored nipples with his thumbs and nuzzles at my neck and ear, sending pulse after pulse of pleasure down my body. I can feel my passion coiling into a tight spring and I rock against him, urging him to take me.

He suckles at my nipples, biting them playfully as I

fumble with his jeans, trying to slide them down. His cock jumps free and I lick my lips at the feel of it. Pushing him off of me, I roll over on top of him and pull his jeans off and run my hands over the silky hair on his body. He has the body of a runner, sinewy but muscular, and I lick a path down to his awaiting gift.

When I get there, I smile up at him, his eyes hooded as he watches me, then slowly, I slide my mouth down the length of him. I suck him as my fist pumps his shaft. Then I twirl the tip in my mouth as I stroke faster. He groans, wrapping his hands in my long hair pushing himself deeper into my mouth until I gag. Over and over again, he slides his cock deep, fucking my mouth and I take him in, my body throbbing in time with his thrusts.

He grabs my hair and pulls me upward to kiss him lightly. He tells me that it is his turn and rolls back over on top of me. He kisses down my stomach making his way to my panties. With my skirt around my waist, he reaches up and slowly pulls my panties down and off. He gradually spreads my legs apart and wide meeting my hot center with his tongue. He grabs my waist and licks my clit with the speed of an Italian R rolling off his tongue, sending a jolt through me as my inner coil winds tighter. As he sucks and licks me, thrusting a finger inside my wetness, I moan for him to take me.

His jaw tightens as he tries to regain control. Sliding his cock up and down my wet slit, I shudder at the feel of it before I position it at my entrance. I look into his eyes and say, "Do you want me?"

He groans, his hands splaying on my breast as he tries to drive into me but I clench my thigh muscles to keep him from gaining entrance, "I've wanted you since I moved to America," he moans.

With a wicked smile, I relax my thighs and allow him to fill me completely as his hips drop. His eyes close and his face contorts into pure ecstasy as I rock my hips back and forth grinding to accommodate his penetration. He begins to move with me, slowly at first before we begin to build up speed.

He slips his hand between us and captures my clit between his fingers. He begins teasing my clit as he thrusts and I begin grinding harder onto him, my moans getting louder and deeper with each thrust. The spiral of need inside me builds and builds with each hard drive until finally, the tight coil springs and I am left screaming and shuddering. My body clenches tightly around his cock and he gives a guttural cry, saying something in Italian, as his hot release spills into me.

He collapses onto my chest, panting and completely satisfied as he brushes my hair from my forehead. He kisses me deeply one last time, leans up on his elbows and asks, "Go out with me?"

"Okay", was the only word my mind and body could coherently form.

With a mischievous look in his eyes he says, "Good. Then I will use my cell to call somebody now to get us out of here...yes?"

23 THE SECRETARY

I flick the light off in my office and make my way towards the elevator. Pausing, I notice the light on in my partner's office. I have no doubt who I will find. My partner mostly worked from the London office, but his secretary was here to keep his office running smoothly. She was more of an assistant than a secretary since she had a master's in business.

All the years that I had known her, I hadn't thought much of her. Sure, she was incredibly sexy with her golden brown hair, deep green eyes and dusty skin. She had a slight accent from studying abroad and she had a long, lean body that she took care of. I don't imagine that she's had a lot of time lately to take care of herself with the late hours my partner has been demanding of her.

Peeking my head in, I take in her attire. She looks comfortable, her bare feet up on the desk, her skirt sliding up her thighs. She had her hair down, flowing around her shoulders and her neat white blouse was unbuttoned to the third button. Her glasses rested on the tip of her nose as she typed on the laptop perched on her lap. She jumps slightly at my voice.

"You're working late again?"

She smiles at me, her eyes sparkling, "Yeah, I get more done when no one bothers me."

Realizing that she just insulted one of her bosses, she says, "I mean, not that you are bothering me..."

I laugh, "Don't worry about it. I know what you meant. I will see you tomorrow and make sure you get security to walk you to your car."

****

As I finish up my work, I stretch and notice that the light in her office is on again. I haven't been able to get the image of her out of my head. She looked amazing last night and I spent the night dreaming about running my hands up her skirt and under it. I imagined her perky breasts in my hands and the taste of her depths on my mouth.

I gather up my things to leave for the night but hesitate. Most people leave early on Friday night but not her. Instead, she was hard at work. Crossing the dark office, I knock on her door. It swings open and I find her standing in the room, her tight black bra is the only thing covering her breasts and her ass is completely bare as she quickly slides on a matching pair of panties. I notice on her desk beside her is a set of gym clothes and I realize that she must have left earlier and had just gotten back from an exercise class.

Not sure what to do, I turn my back to her and ask, "Whoa! What type of class do you take?"

Pink stains her skin and she tries to hide herself. I give her a minute and turn to see her slide behind the chair to block herself. My cock stiffens at the sight of her and I breathe in her scent, which is earthy. "I'm sorry, I didn't think anyone else was here," she says with a tremor in her voice.

I cough and say, "Don't be. I'm sorry too. I didn't mean to barge in; I just wanted to know if you wanted to go for a drink."

She looks at her desk, hesitation clear in her eyes before saying, "Can you give me five minutes?"

I nod and step out of the room, closing the door after me. I try to think of anything except the beautiful woman in the room behind me. A few minutes later, she steps out in her regular skirt and blouse that has become her office attire. On her feet are flip flops and I can't help but notice the cherry red nail polish on her toes. I wonder if her toes will taste as good as they look. Noticing where I am looking, she blushes again and says, "These are all I have, I left my heels in my car."

The ride down the thirty floors to the bar on the main floor is excruciating. All I can think about is her naked body in her office but instead of bringing it up, I ask, "So are you enjoying your work with our firm?"

She nods, "Yes, I love it and with Mr. Adams being in London, I almost feel like my own boss."

She blushes at what she just said, since I am technically her boss too, but I laugh, "Yeah, I guess I don't bother you too often...well, except for last night and tonight."

We head into the bar and sit down at a table out of the way. I catch a waitress's eye and she comes over to take our order. She starts, "Oh, I left my purse upstairs, I'll be right back."

I wave her away, "The drinks are on me...to apologize for barging in."

Heat flares in her eyes and I wonder if it is desire or embarrassment, "Well, if that's the case, I will have a scotch."

She rambles off the brand and I am surprised at the selection, "I would have thought you would order one of those drinks with an umbrella," I say.

"My dad was in the Navy, he introduced me to scotch when I was twenty one and it became our drink. We always shared a scotch at every holiday. He had wanted a boy, but he never got one so he made due with me. He passed away last year."

"I'm sorry to hear that," I say and I realize that I am. She seems like such a sweet woman, I didn't want to see her hurting. I was definitely surprised by her...scotch and being a tomboy was the last thing I would have expected.

"So where did you live as a Navy brat?" I asked, hoping to change the subject.

She launched into her story and I found myself enjoying her company. She smiled often and she would laugh when I said a joke. I couldn't believe it, but I wanted to get to know this woman in more ways than physically. But then again, I wanted to know her physically as well.

As the night wore on, one drink turned into another, which turned into a third. I was just about to order a fourth round when she interrupted me.

"Thanks for the drinks, but I really need to get back to work. Mr. Adams wants a report finished by tomorrow."

Feeling disappointed, I walked her back to the elevator and went up to our office. I stood just behind her and I couldn't help myself, I leaned over and breathed in the scent of her strawberry shampoo. That, combined with the scent of scotch, was a strange mixture that was heady and exciting. Here was a woman I could enjoy knowing.

She leaned back slightly and her ass brushed against my groin. My cock sprung to attention at that small movement but I didn't push her away. Instead, I allowed her to rest against my bulge, aching to press it into her the entire ride.

When the elevator doors slid open, we stepped out. She turned towards me and opened her mouth. I am sure she was going to thank me, but she never got the chance as my mouth covered hers. I kissed her softly, afraid that I would scare her away. She groaned and, to my surprise, she jumped into my arms. I caught her by the ass and she wrapped her legs around my waist. Her warm center rocked against my bulge and I moaned as she deepened the kiss.

As the kiss came to an end, I set her down, completely ready to take her back to my office. She gave me a disappointed look and turned away from me, fleeing into her office.

What just happened? I was positive that she was hot for me, but maybe she thought I was done.

"To hell with that," I said to no one as I walked towards her office. I knocked again before entering, only to find her standing in the office, in just her bra and skirt as she was sliding on a yoga shirt. Spreading the shirt across her chest, she tried to hide her beautiful breasts from me. I crossed the room, not apologizing for barging in and place a searing kiss on her mouth. I could feel her melting into me and I pulled away, "I expect you in the boardroom immediately," I growl.

And with that, I headed towards the boardroom. A few seconds later, she walked in. I saw that she placed her blouse on again. She reached out to turn on the lights in the boardroom, but I captured her arm.

I pulled her into me, the lights still off, and kissed her passionately. At first she didn't respond and then she began kissing me just as fiercely. I ripped open her blouse to find her breasts bare...she had taken her bra off. Groaning, I picked her up and placed her on the table. Lowering my head, I ran my tongue over the tight peaks of her nipples. I sucked one in and she cried out my name, wrapping her legs around me. Lightning shot into my groin and I couldn't wait for her.

I reached under her skirt and found that she wasn't wearing any underwear. Pulling my pants down, I freed my cock and stroked it while she gazed down at it. I spread her legs wide and laid her down on the table. My cock twitched in excitement and I saw her biting her lip as she tried to control her reaction.

Thumbing her clit, I massaged it and she raised her hips to match the speed. When she did, I drove my cock deep inside her. She slid back on the table, so I crawled up onto it, my cock thrusting in and out of her wetness.

She was so slick and tight. She groaned as my cock thrust in and out of her. I felt her rotating her hips, catching my speed and matching my movements. Her nails bit into my ass and I could feel her tighten around my cock. I thrust one last time into her, we both cried out as we reached our peak together.

I collapsed to the side of her on the big table. I drew her into my arms as she whispered to me, "I take Krav Maga."

I laughed at yet another surprise she has revealed. The very fact that I hadn't guessed one thing right about this beauty beside me had my cock growing again. She was amazing. I roll back on top of her, ready to give her a surprise of my own.

24 THE CAVEMAN

I could smell them through the trees, the man and his woman. I had been following them for days through the wilderness, watching them as he tried to win this fierce woman over and she continued to ignore him. I knew why. This woman was mine. Her brown hair hung matted down her back and the furs covered her completely, making her look like a brown lump. But I knew what she looked like, her white skin shining in the cold morning light as she would swim naked, her small breasts and brown nipples perfect for my hands, her slender waist and wide hips making me want to grab her ass.

I tried to ignore this couple as I searched for food but I always found them again. The man was weak, not strong like me. He didn't have my wide shoulders or my muscular body. He didn't deserve her. I watched her follow him at a distance each day knowing he hadn't conquered her yet.

I came across them again at a stream. I sniffed, taking in the scent of her and knew that I had to have her. I came running from the bushes and smacked the man down. He cried out in pain as my violence drove him into the ground. He had what I wanted and I always took what

I wanted. In fear, he scrambled to his feet and ran away. I sneered, such a weakling...he did not deserve this woman.

Turning towards the woman, I see that she has not run. She is grinning at me, her brown eyes searching me. My cock jumps in expectation as it turns hard. I launch myself at her and wrestle her to the ground. Her fist comes up and I see black dots from the force of her blow. My cock swells even larger and I grab her breast through the furs but she bites down on my neck and I find myself roaring in pain.

She breaks free from me before I can conquer her and takes a few steps from me. She keeps her gaze at me and I know I can't take her here. I am puzzled; I always take what I want. I grunt at her to follow and she does.

She follows me every day at a distance as we hunt and she is as fierce as I am. She does not allow me close enough to mount her and my frustration grows with each day. My cock is sore and I stroke it every night with her watching, but she doesn't offer to help me.

I have taken other women and I feel confused by not taking her, but she is a fierce hunter and I find that I enjoy her company. She is angry and she takes her anger out on our prey, beating them as violently as I beat her man. I admire her strength and I still watch her as she bathes, her white skin teasing me.

As the days turn colder, I find us a cave. We store up our food and wood but she still keeps her distance. As winter descends on us, we become trapped in the cave, our small fire keeping us warm.

But tonight, the warmth of the fire is not enough. I want her to warm me and when she falls asleep, I move my pelts to her sleeping area. I slide in behind her, my naked body trembling at the touch of her naked skin. She awakens and her fists fly against my body, bruising it but her violence only makes me smile with need.

Capturing her wrists in my hand, I draw them above her head and lie on top of her. My other hand closes on her breast and I flick her hard nipple. My hand runs down her breast as I lick and bite at her neck. I can feel her struggling and then she begins to soften for me. I let go of her hands thinking she will not fight anymore...

Then pain lances my head and I realize that she has struck me with a large bone. She wriggles out from under me shouting and stands naked against the back of the cave. The bone is clutched between her hands and she looks ready to club me again.

I chuckle at her bravery knowing I will conquer her tonight and carefully stalk her through the cave. She swings the bone at me again and I wrench it from her hands. I shove her against the wall as her legs part. I bite her neck and slide myself along her wet slit. She is ready for me. As I reach down adjusting myself to thrust into her, she wrenches my head back by my hair and wriggles free again.

I growl and begin shouting at her as she tries to run away again. There's nowhere for her to run. I quickly grab her hair and throw her down onto the furs. Landing on top of her, I am not going to let her get away this time. I trap her swinging fists above her head and grind my cock onto her opening. She begins panting and I feel her arch her back. She begins grunting, urging me to enter her.

I smile at her and bite her neck, but I refuse. I let go of her hands and she runs them down my naked back, her fingernails leaving a deep scratch in my skin. My cock is dripping from my excitement, but I can see the lust in her eyes and I won't give in to her. I will take her the way I want to.

With all her force, she rolls me over so she is on top and tries to shove me into her. I pull back and bring her head down so she is on all fours as she bites at my nipples and chest. She reaches up and slaps me across my face in frustration.

I slide out from under her and pin her into this position so she remains on all fours. I grab her hips and press her ass against my hardness and she gasps as I do. She struggles to try to turn but I keep her on all fours. I get a fist of her hair wrapped tightly in my hand and tug it harshly back making her arch her back and with a fierce thrust; I drive myself into her opening as deep as I can.

She screams, but I don't stop. I thrust deeper as she tightens and shudders around me and then I pull out to her opening waiting for her to take what I knew she wanted. She drives her hips back onto me stretching and filling her completely. I let go of her hair, grab her hips and thrust again, harder and deeper. She begins to grunt in pleasure and I continue to drive into her, pulling her hair again, each thrust as violent as the last. Her back arches in pleasure and she meets my violent thrusts by slamming her ass backwards into me.

Her body flutters around me as I work, clutching at it and sucking it deeper. I thrust over and over until my cock bursts and my seed shoots out of me. I can feel her tighten, milking my release, our grunts of passion filling the cave.

I collapse on top of her, forcing her to her stomach as my cock slides out of her. She lifts up on her side throwing me off of her back. I can feel myself getting harder again as she turns to me and roughly pulls my hair whispering, "I...your...woman...now."

25 THE CHEF

"Alyssa, we are in serious trouble," Brian, my assistant said with a flamboyant twist of his arms.

I sighed and glanced up from my checklist for the charity fundraiser. I had been planning this event for a year and as the host, I needed everything to go off without a hitch. The proceeds for the fundraiser gala would be going towards a new building for the children's hospital. Not only would it mean new equipment for the children's wing but the building would be a home away from home for the families of the sick kids.

As far as I knew, all of my i's were dotted and my t's were crossed, I couldn't see anything that would mean serious trouble. Brian was briskly crossing the room towards me, his designer clothes and hair perfect, as he continued to wave his arms around. I sighed again, for Brian, everything was a disaster.

"What's wrong this time?" I ask, unable to keep the irritation from my tone.

"The caterer," he gulped in a breath, "He hasn't shown. I phoned him and he said that he has to cancel. He had a family emergency!"

"What!" I nearly shrieked the word. The floor fell

away from me and Brian quickly grabbed me. "The event starts in three hours, how can we get the meal done in time?"

My chest began to tighten and I struggled to take a breath. Tears stung my eyes and I tried to shake the dizziness that had come over me. "I'm not sure," Brian said as he allowed me to clutch onto him in my distress.

"Hey guys," the voice was strong, masculine and completely familiar.

I glanced up and between my tears; I saw the sandy blonde hair of Corbin, my best friend's brother. "You came," I said and sailed over to him as quickly as I could.

I launched myself into him and marvelled at his strength as he swung me around. He had the body of a line backer and his chiselled good looks were only emphasized by the good natured personality that shone in his ice blue eyes. If I was honest, I had a small crush on him, but the need I was feeling in that instant was not for him but for his skill as a caterer. "What's wrong Alyssa?"

His eyes searched my tear stained face and I realized that I could breathe again. "The caterer cancelled last minute and I have no one else to do the meal. Could you do it? Please, I will pay you double."

"I'm not sure..." Setting me down, he rubbed the back of his neck, "I don't have any staff or any of the supplies..."

"I do," I cut him off. "I can provide you with the supplies and the event hall's kitchen is fully stocked for the meal."

Racing over to my clipboard, I pulled out the menu for the evening. "I have everything to make this meal. Could you make it," I ask as tears fell down my face handing him the menu.

Turning his gaze to the paper, his eyes ran over the list, "Yeah, these are easy but..."

"Please," I beg, wiping my cheeks. After weeks of preparing for this event, I know I look far from sexy but I bite my lip and give him my biggest, hazel puppy dog eyes that I can.

Finally, he says, "Okay, for you. And don't worry about the fee. We'll figure out payment later." He gave me a reassuring hug and kissed me on my forehead.

Wondering what he meant by figuring out the payment later, I let Brian lead Corbin to the kitchen while I finish off the final details for the gala.

Two hours later, everything is as ready as it will ever be. I take one last glance over the ballroom and stage and give myself a pat on the back. The decorations are beautiful, the lighting perfect and the band and guest speaker ready and waiting. Now all we needed was for me to get ready and for the meal to be done.

Entering the kitchen, I smell the delicious food filling the air. Looking around, I see dish after dish being prepared or prepared. Corbin is standing to the side, watching his kitchen staff and looking more handsome than ever before. Seeing me, a lazy smile crosses his boy next door face and I feel my knees weaken. "How is everything coming?" I ask as I walk past him towards the small office in the back.

"We'll be on time and I am positive it will taste better than what your old caterer would have made."

I grin at his cocky attitude as he follows behind me. "Shouldn't you be getting ready Alyssa? I mean, I hope you are not hosting looking like that."

I laugh, and hold up the tight red dress for him to see. His eyes darken as I slip my shirt off, but I ignore it. I have undressed in front of Corbin for years...he was more like a brother...wasn't he? The bulge forming in his pants might say otherwise and he quickly excuses himself before I can slide the dress fully on.

I continue to dress, fix my hair and touch up my makeup. Finally ready for the evening, I leave the office and see him working at one of the stoves. Walking up behind him, I slip my arms around his waist as he turns into me and hug him tightly. Then, for some reason, I reach up and place a chaste kiss on his lips, and murmur sincerely, "You are my saving grace tonight, Corbin."

My mouth burns at the touch and I feel a jolt of electricity wind its way through me. He pulls away and pushes me slightly before grasping my hand. "I changed the dessert and want you to try it before I serve it."

He leads me through the large kitchen to the dessert area and dipped a fork into the chocolate dessert that lined the counter. Slowly, he raised the fork and placed a small bite on my tongue. My eyes shut at the smooth sweetness of the dessert and I couldn't help but moan in pleasure. This dessert was orgasmic, like he had bottled chocolate sin and made it into a dessert.

"That is delicious," I breathed, "What is it called?"

"Uh uh," he whispered against my cheek, raising the hairs on the back of my neck with that same electricity I had felt a moment before. "I will tell you the name of it if we make it through the night." I gazed up in his eyes and wondered at the secrets showing in them.

"Alyssa, guests are arriving," Brian's efficient voice drains the spark from me and I turn towards him.

"Okay, I will be right there," I say before turning to Corbin, "Thanks again Corbin, you are a lifesaver."

And with that, I hurried out the kitchen doors. The evening was a blur of food, entertainment and champagne. Guest after guest praised me about my venue, my decorations and most importantly about my choice of chef. By the end of the evening, Corbin was a household name and his food, including his dessert, opened up the wallets and money was flowing freely for the children's hospital.

Three long hours later, we had met our fundraising goal; in fact, we had surpassed it by at least a million. I was beaming from the success of the night and already had several guests asking me to plan their own parties and galas.

By the time the last guest left, I was exhausted. Entering the kitchen, I found it cleaned and dark. A thread of disappointment wrapped around me as I headed towards the office but then I saw Corbin sitting near the dessert counter.

"I saw that you hadn't eaten," he grinned as I walked up to him, "So I saved you a dessert."

I sighed, "Did I tell you that you're a lifesaver?"

"More than once."

He lifted me up and placed me carefully on the counter. Reaching up, I undid the pins and allowed my red hair to fall around my shoulders. I sighed as he slipped my heels off and started massaging my feet. "Here, eat up."

I picked up the fork and took a bite of the chocolate dessert. It was as wonderful as the first bite early today. Corbin's chuckle made me open my eyes, "You have a little bit of chocolate here."

He leaned in and kissed the corner of my mouth, licking the chocolate from it. I shuddered under his lips and he shifted his mouth slightly to form his lips to mine. His kiss was deep and passionate, but I could feel him holding back. His arms under my hands shook and I could feel his hard shaft against my knee. When we were both breathless, he broke the kiss and said, "Here, let me."

Nudging my legs apart, he stands between them and grabs the dessert. Spooning another bite into my mouth, he watches me as I lick the chocolate off of the fork. Bite after bite, he feeds me, his eyes darkening and the bulge in his pants pressing harder against me. I shift to ease the pulse down below and brush against his hardness. Electricity shoots through me at the feel of it against me and my hazel eyes fill with need.

Corbin sets the empty plate down and leans towards me. His hands rest on my hips and I feel like he is burning me with them. "I'm going to kiss you again," he purrs.

My mouth goes dry and I watch his lips descend

towards me, aching for them like I have never done before. They sear my mouth as his tongue teases my lips then they sear a path down my jaw to my neck. His hands kneed my hips, rocking his hard shaft against my clit barely covered by my satin panties and I find myself panting as I fight the orgasm building inside of me.

I unbutton his chef's jacket and loosen his pants, sliding them down his legs. His cock juts forward, up to his tight stomach and I can see it weeping. I lick my lips and he lifts me from the counter and turns me around. Slowly, he unzips my dress and allows it to fall to the ground. His hands slide over my back before he undoes my bra and then he trails kisses down my back and over my ass as he slips my panties off. I am left standing there, shaking with need, in nothing but my red stilettos.

Turning me back around, he reaches onto the counter and brings out a small bottle of chocolate sauce. Lifting me up, he places me back on the counter and drips a small drop of chocolate onto my nipple. Licking it off, I jerk at the way he is suckling my nipple. He covers the other nipple with chocolate and licks it clean. Returning to my mouth, he kisses me deeply, our tongues twining together. All I can taste is him and chocolate and that bolt of electricity shoots right to my clit.

He grins as he kisses down my body, dribbling chocolate as he does. He coats my clit in the chocolate and with one, heated glance at me, he licks and sucks intensively. I cry out in pleasure and wrap my legs around his head as he laps up the chocolate. I am close to orgasm when he stands up and in one swift movement, pulls me off the counter, bends me over and plunges deep inside me.

His own cry has me bucking against him, drawing him deeper and deeper. Reaching around to stroke my clit as his hard and fast thrusting pushes me over the edge, his body begins to shake along with mine and with a final thrust, we are riding our orgasms together – both of us screaming our pleasures into the darkness.

Falling against my back, wrapping his arms around me, I bring his hand up to my mouth. As I lick the last of the chocolate from his finger, I hear him chuckle and say, "It's called Chocolate Orgasm," then pulls me to the floor.

26 THE CHEERLEADER

She is there and I can't draw my eyes from her. She is beautiful in her short cheerleading skirt and half top. I watch her as she shakes her pom-poms and I want to wave at her but I don't. Instead, I try to look at the other girls in the group. A small football hits me in the head and I look over to find her laughing at me as the other cheerleaders throw small footballs in the crowd.

I can't help thinking about this morning when I ran into her. I had been out running, the IPod playing in my ear as I start out. I didn't see her and she didn't see me until she was crashing into me. I fell to the ground and her lithe body had tumbled down on me. I felt her tight body press against me and her perfect breasts pressed against my hard chest. I had wanted to smother her in kisses as her scent filled my senses.

She had clumsily gotten up, but not before noticing how hard my shaft had gotten. Then she ran off, disappearing before I could even get her name. I ignored my run and went back into the hotel room to have a cold shower.

For the rest of the day, the Saturday night college football game we were waiting to see didn't dull the excitement I had for the blonde hair nymph that had captured my imagination.

And there she was, dancing on the field for halftime. Then she disappears into the crowd and the game resumes. I can't get her off my mind but soon the football game draws me into it. Our team is behind by three but in the last thirty seconds of the game, the quarterback throws a Hail Mary touchdown to the end zone. We go wild at the win and I find myself pulled along with the crowd.

As I glance towards the field, I am disappointed by the fact that the blonde cheerleader is gone. Still, there is always a chance that I can see her again at the hotel.

I head back with my friends and as we enter the bar, Tim, my best friend says, "Hey, let's go and celebrate with the team in the bar."

We all head into the bar and find an empty area at the end of the bar. The place is packed with the team and fans that had driven up to watch the game. As I look around the bar, I see her, standing with a group of girls...all of them cheerleaders. She looks bored but as she turns to look around, her blue eyes slide over me. She smiles and I watch her slide through the crowd, her hips swaying to the music. She is still wearing the cheerleading uniform from earlier and I would love to see her out of it. I feel my erection growing even before she grins and leans into me, "I've been looking for you all night," she purrs into my ear.

"I've been looking for you," I reply, my hand brushing her back as I do.

She stares at me, desire filling her eyes and I fight the urge to run my tongue down her neck. "Well, now that you have found me, what are you going to do to me?"

Before I can answer, Tim laughs and says, "Hey, aren't you the pretty little cheerleader who knocked Jack on the head with a football?"

She laughs and it is a throaty laugh that brings to mind dark bedrooms and nights of passion. She nods, "Yeah, I didn't think anyone noticed. Nice to meet you," she holds out her hand.

"Tim and you know Jack obviously," Tim shakes her hand and then she extends her hand to me. I take it and the heat I feel is instant. I want this woman desperately and all I can think about is my cock sliding into her.

I spend the next hour chatting with her as we enjoy drink after drink. She fetches the occasional item for the bartender, who she happens to know, before she goes back to flirting with me. Occasionally, she rubs her body against me and I can't help but respond to her. I want to take her up to my room and strip her naked, but I hesitate, not sure if she will be interested.

"Hey, I have to grab some beer from the store room for Darryl, the bartender. Could you come and help me?" she asks, leaning into me.

I grin and nod. Maybe now is the time.

Reaching the store room, I enter before her and turn around to see her locking the door behind her. I take a swallow of my beer in hand and watch her as she walks across the room towards me.

"I've seen you watching me all night. What were you thinking?"

"How sexy you are in your cheerleading outfit," I answer.

She grins and moves towards a shelf. She bends down low and I catch a flash of her panties under the short skirt. She reaches under her skirt and slides her panties off and I can't stop my heart from racing in excitement. "Well, here you go big guy," she says, slipping the panties into my pocket, "So you can keep thinking about how sexy this outfit is."

She grabs a case of beer and puts it in my arm before turning towards the door and unlocking it. "We better get this beer out front, before they come looking for us."

I follow her out, but all I can think about is her bare ass under that skirt. Her panties burn through my jeans and I fight the urge to pull them out and smell her scent. She spends the next half hour rubbing against me and making sure that I remember she isn't wearing any panties. My cock feels like it is about to burst and I finally give up. I need to get to my hotel room to stroke out the tension I am feeling.

As I stand up, she says, "Hey, can you help me in the store room again?"

I nod and follow her, wondering how she was going to tease me again. When I enter the store room, I hear her lock the door again. I turn around and see her facing the door. Her hands shake and I move over to her. I run my hands down her silky skin and I feel her shiver under me. I move her long blonde hair off of her neck, kissing it when it is bare.

She moans and presses her ass into my cock and I feel dizzy at the passion running through me. She murmurs, "You have shown remarkable restraint tonight," as she turns in my arms.

Her hands work feverishly at my belt and she slips my pants and underwear down. My cock springs free and her hand is around it, pumping it as I grind my teeth together to prevent from coming in her hand. I turn her around so my cock can nestle in her ass crack. I can feel her hot flesh sucking at my cock and she groans as she pushes against me.

She leans over and places one foot on the shelf. My cock slides easily into her pussy and then she is gripping my long shaft with her muscles. I moan at how hot and wet her tightness is and I pull her closer against me as I wrap my arms around her waist.

I pump into her several times as the need builds in me. Hearing her moan, I reach under her skirt and massage her clit. She begins writhing under me, screaming in passion as her orgasm explodes around my cock and then I am exploding into her, shooting out all of me, deep inside her. As I feel the last drop being wrung from my cock by her clenching muscles, I groan and ask, "What are you going to put in my pocket this time?"

She leans her head back and laughs, "Nothing, but I could use your help again if you're up to it … in my hotel room."

27 THE MARINE

Another day at the airport and I was tired as I shuffled through security. Slipping my feet out of my shoes, I put them in the bin and walked through the security check for what seemed like the tenth time this week. The airport was fairly quiet; I was taking the redeye home.

Gathering up my things on the other side of the gate, I take a step back and bump into a hard wall of flesh. I gasp and drop my shoes and carryon luggage as I try to keep from falling. I turn around and come eye to eye with the brightest blue eyes I have ever met. They burned into me and I had a hard time turning away from him.

Heat coursed through me and my gaze slipped down to his full, plump lips and the small dimple in his cheek as he smiled. I looked down lower and saw the blue dress uniform of the marines but it did nothing to hide his firm body from my perusal.

Bending down, I noticed that his short cropped hair was black and dusted with silver. His large hands reached out and he began helping me pick up my stuff, "I am so sorry..." I gushed, "I am such a klutz."

He chuckled and the sound wrapped around me. "Don't worry about it, I was partly to blame."

He passed me my stuff and I gave him a small smile,

"So where are you headed?"

"Back to the base in Texas, you?"

I couldn't help but grin at my fortune, "I'm heading to Texas as well."

And with that, we waved goodbye and he walked away to the waiting area while I went in search of a good tea. After taking a few steps, I quickly turn around and yell, "Hey – thanks for your service!"

He turned back to me and gave me a huge smile and I felt myself melt right to the floor. Heat flooded my cheeks and spread lower as I felt a startling amount of desire roar through me.

After gathering up my tea, I headed to the gate and saw him resting against the window, his head resting on it and his eyes closed. Looking around, I saw that we were alone but I decided not to disturb him. Instead, I sat ten feet away and opened up my laptop to check my email.

As I was answering the fourth email, I jumped when he said, "Most people don't work at this time of night."

I looked up and found him sitting directly across from me. Grinning I said, "How do you know I am working? Maybe I am sending an email to my lover."

"Really, tell me I'm wrong and that you are sending something naughty to some lucky guy."

I laughed and it eased all the tension of my business trips this week, "Okay, you got me. I was working."

"You know, that isn't good for you. What is good for you though is to talk to me," he said and winked.

I took him up on his offer and began chatting to him. He was from a small town in Ohio, but was stationed in Texas. He had been in the marines for five years and was moving up in the ranks. I talked about how I had grown up in Texas and spent a lot of time travelling for work. The talk was pretty light, just small details about where we came from and that we were both single.

By the time the gate attendant called out that we could board the plane, I had warmed to this marine, and his name was Colin.

When we boarded, I noticed that I was five rows away from him so I decided to take a chance and move to the seat beside him. "Oh, I'm going to report you for breaking the rules," he teased, his eyes twinkling.

"I don't think they will mind," I said, grinning back at him, "There is no one else on the plane tonight. Besides, six hours is an awful long time to be sitting alone."

He nodded his head and we talked a bit more as the plane shuttled onto the runway and took off. When we were in the air, the flight attendant came by and we ordered drinks. After we were settled in with drinks in our hands, the flight attendant said, "We will be in the back if you need anything, just press the button."

I nodded, my grin becoming mischievous as I watched her close the curtain behind her. The lights in the cabin were dim. "You know, they are going off to sleep," I said.

"Probably, it is what I would do."

I laughed, "Yeah, but instead, you are stuck talking to me. Should I move back to my seat so you can get some sleep?"

I made to get up and he caught my hand. My flesh felt seared where he touched me and I gasped at my instant reaction to him. "No, I want someone to talk to. I'm not tired at all."

I sighed in longing and winked at him, "You're not trying to convince me to join the mile high club are you?"

"Are you kidding, have you seen how big those bathrooms are? I have no interest in screwing in one of those stalls."

"Really," I purred, "We could get into some tight positions in the bathroom."

He grinned and leaned in towards me, whispering, "Oh, I am sure that you are plenty tight."

I groaned at the fire licking through me. I breathed in a sigh and say, "I have to admit but I am completely turned on right now. I would love to show you just how tight I really am."

He stiffened and I looked down to see the huge bulge in his pants. I ran my hand over his bulge and he sucked air between his teeth. "I can be really quiet," I purred and placed a kiss on his neck.

He looked back at the curtain, uncertainty in his eyes, "Trust me, they're asleep and we don't need much room."

I shifted up and slid onto his lap, my knees on either side of his lap. "We have a few hundred square feet to get our position just right for this mile high club."

Desire lit his eyes and I licked his ear. I unbuttoned his jacket and placed it on the seats in the center aisle. Standing up, I slid my underwear off and sat back down on him, positioning my skirt to cover us. I kissed his jaw and moved up to his lips. I took my time as I slowly kissed him. He deepened the kiss and took over my mouth. I groaned quietly as he did, rocking my hips and rubbing myself on him. I lifted up as he slid down his pants and then I settled against his hard length.

He groaned as my slit rubbed against him. He pulled open the front of my shirt, pushed my bra up and sucked my nipple into his mouth. I slid my hand between us and slowly guided him into my wet depths. I lowered myself until he was buried deep inside me.

Moaning into my breasts, he pinched my nipple and I jerked on his cock, drawing a groan from both of us. I rocked back and forth as he slid his hands under my ass. Then he lifted me up and down his length and my eyes rolled back into my head as my center tightened around his shaft.

He thrust into me again and again and the tension built in me. I was moaning softly and he captured my moans with his mouth as I shuddered in my climax, barely able to stay quiet. A second later, I was capturing his moans with my mouth as he came deep inside me. We both shook in the aftermath of our orgasms and as I slumped against his shoulder. We heard the flight attendant rattling her cart knowing she was going to come offer us more drinks. I jumped off of him and we hurriedly put ourselves back together. I didn't have time to get my shirt all the way buttoned, so I took his coat and covered myself like a blanket just in time to see the flight attendant push her cart next to us and offer us more drinks. I laughed under my breath at our heavy breathing and ordered water and he ordered water as well. As the flight attendant was walking away, she turned to lay her arm on his shoulder.

"Thank you for your service," she said with a genuine smile and walked off. I looked over at him and he laughed. Then I laid my head on his shoulder and sighed, "Yes, thank you for your service."

28 THE WARLORD

The skin on my wrists and ankles was quickly rubbed raw by the iron shackles that encircled them. I tried to move them as gently as possible; the pain was becoming more than I could bear. Silent tears coursed down my cheeks as reality sank into my soul. I was going to be sold, like a beast of burden in the market square.

My angry thoughts turned to my mistress, who had turned her wrath upon me for refusing to lay with a man I despised. She had pulled me from my kitchen duties with a cold stare and shouted, "Come with me now, Anna." I was led to his chambers, her curt smile telling me exactly what she expected of me. I was hurt and confused as to why Mistress suddenly gave me to this man. She had always promised to keep me protected. But her eyes were empty, I didn't know this woman. I hesitated and looked up at her pleadingly. I thought she had loved me. I was told to undress and present myself to this vile man who I knew had slain many of my countrymen. My dress fell to the floor as my mistress left the room.

I could still feel his noxious breath heating my skin as leaned in close to my neck and breasts; his heavy panting a sign of what he thought was to come. His beady eyes stared with lust at my most private of places, while drool dripped from the corner of his blood-crusted mouth. Licking his lips, he slowly ran a gnarled finger over my nipple, causing me to shudder in disgust.

The thought of such a creature entering my body filled me with dread, so much so that I ran from his grasping and gnarled fingers. He shouted in anger at my flight and I barely made it to the doors of the great hall before guards overpowered my shaking body. Mistress was displeased. Master Bleeks, as he was called, was an ally and was never to be turned away by anyone, especially by a slave.

I have always lived my life with virtue and have felt the lusty gaze from more than one man, and I was frightened of what the future held for me now. It seemed my long blonde hair and large breasts were attractive to many. My dark blue eyes seemed to carry my innocence inside them which brought more than enough advances from those who preyed on the weak, such as the guards. But I had always belonged to the Mistress. I was hers. I was supposed to be untouchable.

Now, here I was, in a dirty stone-walled cell after being led down a long corridor with other slaves who had the same look of despair on their bleak faces. The cell was tiny and I was shivering with fright. My body was aching from the pain of sitting for so long and the shackles were heavier than the granite that was mined from the hillside. An explosion rocked the building not much longer after I had been thrown into this cramped cell and much shouting could be heard from the small window above me. I didn't care. Let them all burn and be destroyed. My captors cared nothing for me or the other prisoners.

It seemed the attack had lasted hours or more before a commanding voice rang loudly in the air, informing the prisoners that we were to be taken to the courtyard. A tall guard in velvet hat entered the dusty room and one sat his eyes upon me. He swiftly walked towards me and grabbed me up by my arms and forced me to me feet. I, along with the rest of the prisoners, was herded in like cattle to the courtyard to face our fate.

I was last to be asked about my crime. I didn't care what happened next when I spit out furiously, "I am being sold for a crime that I should not have had to commit! I refused to sleep with Lord Bleeks. I have nothing to do with this place."

A hush fell over the crowd and from the looming distance, a man stepped through. He was large, muscled, yet lean. His tan skin was covered with the tribal tattoos of his land. His heavy footsteps seemed to pound in my ears as he approached me. His piercing gaze was electrifying as it held my own. He knelt down in front of me and asked, "Why did you deny a man that was up until an hour ago going to be named King?"

His voice was so kind that I replied honestly, "I refuse to lay with a man I despise." He paused, then smiled, and mentioned to a warrior near him to unshackle my limbs and take me to his new quarters in the tower.

I shakily stood after the weight from the iron circlets was removed. I walked gingerly upon my sore ankles as I was led up many stairs to a lavish room. The warrior kindly smiled as he told me that I was to bathe in the large tub that was sitting beside a roaring fire. He quietly shut the door as I made my way to the bath. I nervously disrobed and stepped into the hot water, the raw skin of my ankles making me wince. I was luxuriating in the scented water as the dirt from the last twelve hours washed away from my delicate skin.

I climbed out of the tub and wrapped myself in a soft cotton sheet that had been set upon the stool next to the tub. I wrapped it around my still-wet body and walked to the large window, viewing the devastation that lay before me from the attack. I knew now what this warlord wanted from me. I felt completely numb, knowing what my fate was.

I was startled when he spoke. His deep voice boomed

through my thoughts. "I know of your people. I am Medeo. I come from the East and have fought many battles against the enemies of those who are dear to you." I had heard of this great warlord that now stood behind me, yet his legendary tales seemed but a myth. He pulled me away from the window and sat me on the bed, offering me a bowl of bright purple grapes and a carafe of water. I drank and ate hungrily as he told me tales of his past. He was interrupted by another warrior's knock on the large wooden door. Medeo excused himself to speak with his comrade and left me to wonder what his ploy was.

He didn't knock before sauntering into the room, the look of calm in his face gone. He stared at my small frame as I sat on the fine linens. My heart started racing. He approached me with a fierceness I had not seen before, his relaxed demeanor gone. I held the sheet closer to my body.

"You had a successful victory today my Lord, but I'm not afraid of you."

He grabbed me up and pushed me against the wall holding me by my throat. He stopped and looked at me viciously speaking, "You should be." Fear entered my body at his actions. "You were her lover." It wasn't a question, but an accusation. Tears stung my eyes and I nodded my head yes. "Have you ever been with a man?" he asked as he tightened his grip. I shook my head no. "And what pray tell, would you do if I brought the Mistress into this room and fucked her in front of you?" I knew he expected a jealous violent reaction from me, but I simply whispered, "I would take your sword and kill her as she is spread beneath you."

Surprise and satisfaction gleamed in his eyes and he let me go. My heart let its barrier down just a bit as he softly stepped back. His eyes were mesmerizing. They held a deep knowledge of the unknown and a wicked flame that made me nervous yet excited. I held his gaze and then dropped my eyes to his bulging forearms and lean sinewy thighs. A fire leaped into my loins, a fire that I had not experienced before in my young life.

Medeo turned his back to me and walked towards the bath. He swiftly undressed and slipped into the tub, his eyes closing softly, enjoying the heat on his sore muscles. I watched him wash himself with the deftest of hands. He ordered me to sit in the chair next to the bath.

"Tell me about your Mistress."

I took a deep breath and began speaking. "I was on my way to Brigadear when my transport was attacked by her rebels. I was captured and taken to her, it was a full moon. She said she was captivated by my beauty and I was sent to her from the gods. The first night I was ordered to bath and dress and then I was taken to a large room filled with mattresses. I was ordered to strip and to lie down. Then the Mistress walked into the room and headed for me. She began caressing my body and doing things to me that I had never experienced before. She spread my legs and inserted a finger. When she knew I had never lain with a man before, she ordered me hers and untouchable."

I looked at him then, his anger had subsided. "Every month on the full moon she would summons me to have sex with her. Not long ago she began acting differently. Last month when I was summoned, she had guards with her. It was unusual because all the other times we were alone. They held my legs apart and she declared that she would be the one to take my virginity and inserted an instrument inside me. She wiped my virgin blood across her face and shouted to the gods that she would look young forever."

Medeo emerged from the water gleaming with droplets of the oil-scented water, and stepped out. His cock was large and hard and the sight of it took my breath away. "Then she tried to give you away," he said in anger. He walked over to me completely naked still wet from the bath.

"Where does your loyalty lie?" he demanded. I

quivered as he stared at me with his question.

The silence was deadening as I stared straight back at his dark and unwavering face, "My loyalty is to myself, Medeo. I allow no one to take me without my permission." I stated. Then I stood up and dropped the sheet away from my body, allowing him to see all of me.

He reached out for my hand, which I gave. He pulled me toward the bed and stared at my nudeness. He softly put his fingers upon my skin and circled by body, tracing every part of me; my stomach, my back, and my behind. His fingers felt like rough feathers, making the deepest part of my womanhood swell with sensation. His fingertips softly touched my nipples, causing them to become erect. Noticing what he was doing to my supple body, he smiled at me.

I knew then that I had to have more of what this man was offering to me. I looked him in his eyes and said, "How do you want me, my warlord?"

He pushed me onto the bed, exposing all of me and answered, "Like this, always like this." His fingers delicately traced every inch of my body. My breasts were swollen and he gently pinched my nipples, causing me to buck my pelvis forward. I was getting so wet between my legs that I couldn't help but splay them. He whispered, "Not yet, my sweet," and began applying gentle kisses to my inner thighs, causing me to moan.

He stood up and stared at my writhing body before swiftly grabbing my hips, forcing his large member at my entrance, his eyes begging the question. I thrust onto him and felt the pain and pleasure in every fiber of my being and didn't want him to ever stop. His driving slowed as he gently pushed in and out of me, both of us indulging in the electrifying friction. Without warning, he rolled over onto his back, pulling my pulsating body with it. I knew what he wanted me to do; I rode this glorious dark warlord like a queen, throwing my long hair back behind me as I pounded up and down his wet swollen sword, impaling myself upon it to its end. I felt myself on the verge of an explosion when my conquered warlord reached his hand forward, rubbing me so intimately that I began breathily screaming in ecstasy. He grabbed my hips and drove upwards hard and fast pumping his seed inside me sending me into an abyss of ecstasy as our moans and screams wakened the night. I calmed myself long enough to lean over onto his sweat-covered chest to whisper into his ear, "Another successful victory, my Lord."

29 THE ALIEN

The thin nightgown clings to my body as the hot air presses me to the bed. Groaning, I turn over and squeeze my eyes shut, trying to will myself to sleep but the hot summer night is making the room overbearing. I wipe the sweat from my face and stare out the window, counting the stars shining brightly over the desert landscape.

Sighing, I swing my legs over the edge of the bed and rub away the sweat on my neck. The heat is the only negative side to living alone here. Moving to the window, I open it but the air outside is as still as the air in the room. Even the overhead fan is doing nothing to create a breeze.

With one last longing look at the bed, I slip down the stairs and out the front door. The quiet of the night washes over me and I don't feel as hot as before even though it is still sweltering. I glide over to the hammock that I have tucked among my favorite desert plants and settle in to it. This isn't the first night that I have spent out here and I feel myself drifting to sleep as I gaze up at the stars.

One star shines brightly in the sky and I feel myself getting sleepier as it grows larger and brighter. I try to look away from the brightness and fall to slumber but I suddenly realize that I can't move. My arms and ankles are pressed to the side of a hard mattress and strapped into place. A mattress?

Oh my god, where am I? I glance around but all I can see are shadows just outside of the light above me. Was I hurt? Am I in a hospital? The sharp smells of antiseptic burn my nostrils and I fight down the acid burning its way up my throat. "Where am I?" The question is a whisper and no one seems to notice. I see a shadow of someone working in the room but they don't answer me.

Taking a deep breath, I try to calm my nerves. Something must have happened but I am in a hospital and everything is going to be okay, I reassure myself. My skin feels as though it is hypersensitive and I can feel my cotton nightgown sliding up. Cool air raises goose bumps on my skin as my lower body is exposed to the person in the room.

"Am I hurt?" My voice sounds pleading.

"It's okay," a masculine voice echoes out of the shadow and my body relaxes at the calm authority in his tone. "All you need to do is relax while I run a few tests."

The questions flee out of my head and I feel my face redden at the reaction that his voice is having on me. Heat spikes up my body and I feel a longing for his touch. What is wrong with me? I'm obviously hurt, I think to myself. Fear courses through me once again at how surreal this all feels. My reaction is that I am not remembering how I got here. The stranger was standing just outside the light, "Why can't I see you?"

"To keep you safe."

His words send terror through me and I start to struggle at the straps, trying to free myself from this prison. I thrash my head back and forth, tears stinging my eyes as I ask, "Are you going to hurt me?"

"No," his voice prickles against my skin again and I flush as heat spreads through me cutting through my fear, "All you have to do is relax, and you'll be able to return home soon."

I take a deep, calming breath and stop fighting the restraints but I can still feel my heart fluttering in my chest. "Just relax," his voice is almost hypnotic and I feel his hands continue sliding my nightgown up.

"Wait," I shudder as the brush of his fingertips lingers on my legs. "Is there anyone in there with you? I can't make out your face, but I see shadows," I couldn't quite focus, were those hands or tentacles?

His touch deepens as it slides across my stomach, sending flutters of nervousness with it but combined with those flutters is an ache that descends between my legs. I feel a gush of wetness between my thighs as he purrs, "No, it's just the two of us. Now just relax while I run my tests."

His voice wraps around me, I breathe in a light mist that is heating me from the outside in and I find myself relax into it. I ignore where I am, the bright light above me, and the fear that I have no idea who or what this man is. Instead, I give myself to the longing that is growing between my legs as I arch up as far as the restraints will allow me. The straps bite into my flesh but it feels erotic and exciting…knowing that I could be taken this way.

His hands hover under my breasts and they feel enormous on my body. His cold wet finger slips over one nipple and I rock back towards the mattress as both nipples pebble in pleasure. They feel rock hard and I can see his shadow bend over me through my eyelashes. Those *are* tentacles behind the dark circle in the middle, why am I not screaming? A tongue dampens the end of one nipple and I close my eyes as I fight my restraints in an effort to hold it over my breast. Unable to do what I want, I arch my chest towards him and hear a chuckle before something sucks at my nipple. His mouth?

I feel something else suck my other nipple and I jerk at the feeling. "Don't worry," he murmurs against my skin, cooling the heated flesh, "We are alone."

My mind races, knowing he doesn't have two mouths. What is this being and what does it want from me. I breathe in another gust of light mist and I no longer care that there is something sucking on both of my nipples as I writhe in ecstasy under my unknown captor. I feel his tentacles slip down my stomach, tracing it with a lazy speed that has me curling my toes in enjoyment, as another set of tentacles caress over my neck. I feel like every part of me is being touched and tickled. A tentacle slides over my neck and I feel suckling on my ear causing me to shudder. The tension between my legs grows as this strange, yet wonderful, thing plays my body until it is as tight as a string. I feel ready to break apart as the straps pull at my arms and ankles, keeping me from moving despite my struggling under them.

I feel a tug at my underwear and then they are ripped from my body, cut away by some instrument I can't see, as something long and cold slides along my inner thigh. Tentacles gently wrap around my ankles while two more push my knees out wide open and I groan; squeezing my eyes shut at all the sensations running over me. Then all touching to my body stops. Fear starts to increase as I'm tied to this mattress, completely naked and my knees spread apart fully exposing my lower body when I breathe in another gust of mist. I calm again when something licks up and down my slit sending a rush of fire through my body and I moan. Inside my body, I feel at odds. Part of me is nervous about all that is happening but the other part wants it to happen.

I gasp as the suction on my nipples and neck resume and then grow stronger. Tentacles run down my bent legs.

My own body betrays me when I feel him blow on my clit. The suction on my body stops again, but the tentacles still roam across me as he licks me again, tasting my wet slit.

A strangled groan filled with agony and arousal fills the room as he sucks my clit and gently nibbles. I realize that the groan is mine. I feel tortured, I don't want this pleasure, but I don't want him to quit. I long for the orgasm that is there, just hovering out of reach and I want him to finish what he is doing, but he doesn't give in.

It's like he can read my mind as he moves away from me. My clit tingles from a vibration that plays against it but I can't tell if it is from my excitement or if he is still touching it. He releases my ankles and spreads my legs wider, tentacles still holding me down, and calming me with their massage. I feel something large slide up and down my slit and over my vibrating clit. "Please, just finish it," I stutter as the suction on my nipples begins again and I feel so close to coming undone. The tension from my unfulfilled orgasm rocks my body and I feel tears slipping from my eyes in a combination of frustration and fear.

"Relax," he purrs against my ear and I feel a new vibration at the opening of my ass combined with the one on my clit. I tense, but his purrs wipe the fear from me. I feel him adjusting over me and I arch my hips to meet him when something thrusts into me. My mouth opens in a silent scream as inch after inch of him grows to stretch me completely. He pulls out of me completely before he thrusts in again...hard...fast. I can barely breathe as the vibrations wash over me and he continues to thrust.

"Stop, oh please, end this!" I beg, the orgasm is so close. Just there out of reach and I close my eyes, focusing on him thrusting into me, focusing on the tendrils of vibrations on my clit and ass, focusing on the suction on my nipples and the tentacles running over me.

I can hear his labored breathing and I buck under him as he groans. His release shoots inside me, a liquid heat that pushes me over the edge and I tumble into an abyss as wave after wave of pleasure spasms against his penetration. The orgasm is nothing I have ever felt before as I scream my satisfaction into the shadowed room.

I feel him slide out of me pulling my nightgown back

down. My eyes slowly start to close; my fear completely gone in the glow of my satisfaction. I give up the fight and allow myself to lay there, sleep slipping over me and as I am drifting into sleep, I hear him whisper, "You can return home now."

30 THE GLADIATOR

The noise of the crowd filled the arena and I ignored them. The man lay before me, his life's blood draining from his body as he stared lifelessly up at the sky. "I'm sorry," I mutter to my friend.

Since I had come to the gladiator ring, we had been best friends. He had trained me in the art of the trident and I had returned the favor with the sword and shield. We were well matched but we always knew that it would come down to this, life or death in the arena.

I moved towards the gates, ignoring the chant of the crowd, Kadius! Kadius! Kadius! It was time to enjoy my victor's rewards.

****

I could hear the crowd from the bath under the arena and my body shivered in terror. Kadius was the victor, a cruel barbarian with dark hair, dark eyes and a terrifying physique. Would he break me as he rode me? I wondered as more honey milk was poured over my ivory shoulders.

The nameless slaves pulled me from the bath and dried me. Then they sat me on a stool and combed my hair until it fell in golden waves down my back. They carefully painted my face with gold and coal and dusted gold across my skin.

Wrapping me in a thin white wrap, they left my feet bear. I felt naked under the material and I couldn't help myself when I closed my arms around my chest trying to hide. A hand snaked out and slapped my hands away...I was the gift and the gift should never show anything but wanting.

I follow the slaves into a large bath room to find the victor entering at the same time. He is even larger in person, standing at least six foot five, his wide shoulders shining with sweat, his muscled chest covered in blood. My knees shake in fear and I feel the urge to run. Before I can, the hand pushes me forward and I hear the voice of my master, "For the champion."

Kadius's eyes narrow at the challenge I must present and he looks at me with sorrow in his eyes. Embarrassment brings color to my cheeks as I realize that I am not good enough for him. I have no idea that he just killed his best friend. "Leave us," he says in an arrogant voice and the room empties, all except for Kadius and I.

I stand in the center of the room, watching as he turns his back to me. He removes his armor and I gasp at the angry scars covering his back. Scars from where the whip beat him into submission...scars from when he rose up and became the strongest Gladiator Rome had ever known. Seeing those scars, my fear is replaced with longing. I want to smooth away those scars with my kisses.

He turns to me and catches the longing on my face but he ignores it again. He steps into one of the baths and begins to rinse away the blood. His skin glows as he scrubs off the dirt and grime and then he moves to the center bath. He stares at me as he bathes, his fist closing around his shaft and I notice that he is hard as he rubs himself back and forth.

I reach up to the clasp at my neck and undo the wrap.

It tumbles to the floor as I step out of it, completely naked. For some reason, I don't feel the fear that I had before as I walk towards the bath. His eyes are guarded and I can't tell if he finds me attractive or not. Only his erection gives any indication that he is aroused.

"You don't have to," he says, his voice full of some unknown emotion, "It is only us here, you do not have to bathe me."

Surprised at his concern for me, I shake my head as I gather up my heavy hair and wind it with the leather straps I had wrapped around my wrist, "They are watching. If I don't oblige, they will kill me."

I step into the bath as he ducks his head under. I can see him cleaning the gore from his hair and when he comes out of the water, beads slide down his face and mark his body. It is beautiful; I realize and question why I was scared of him before.

I gather up the wash rag and run it over his chest to clean him. I can feel the heat rising off of him and I fight the urge to press my body to that heat. I slip the cloth down his stomach and over his legs, avoiding the long shaft jutting up to his stomach. I move around to his back and clean his back, tracing each scar as I do. Hesitating slightly, I kiss the puckered scars and I feel him shudder at my touch.

As the cloth reaches his shoulders, he forcefully grabs my wrist and pulls me around to face him. I can feel his manhood pressing into me and I can't help the fear that traps me to him. I was so sure, but now my virginity has made me lose the confidence that I had earned.

"You don't have to lie with me."

I shake my head tears stinging my eyes, "Yes, I do. They will be waiting for my virgin blood," I pulled away from him and gather up my wrap, spreading it out on the edge of the bath. I turn back, the water tickling my waist and remove the tie from my hair, shaking out the golden waves.

"You are beautiful," he murmurs as he moves towards me.

Capturing a strand of my hair, "You have a fiery spirit. I do want you." His other hand wraps around my breast and his thumb flicks my rosy nipple.

I tense at his touch, not sure to do with the liquid fire that is spreading through me at his touch. I feel like he is burning me. "Don't worry, I won't hurt you," he says, his eyes full of torment, before bending his neck and sucking my nipple into his mouth.

His hand slides down my body, lighting a fire under my skin everywhere he touches me. I cry out as the passion envelopes me and I feel him thumb through the curls at the apex of my thighs. The entire time his fingers explore me, he sucks and licks at first one nipple and then the other. He lifts me from the water and places me on the white wrap.

"Lie down," he commands and I lay back, watching him through my golden eyelashes, my hands fluttering across my stomach as I try to calm my nerves.

He kneels down in the water and places my legs on his shoulders. I shake my head, unsure of what he is going to do. He smiles and blows air across my womanhood. I jerk at the pulse of pleasure that shoots through me. He chuckles as I try to close my legs and forces them open. "Just relax, you will enjoy this," he purrs and then he laps at my slit like a cat licking cream.

I jolt upright, but his hands force me back down and then I can't stop as my legs close around his head. He sweeps his tongue up and down, flicking my clit before he slides it inside my tight hole. I feel a gush of liquid warmth and his breath cools the hot flesh that he is licking. I can't help but relax into a pool of pleasure under his careful ministrations.

I feel him shift slightly and then his finger is sliding up and down my wet slit. I stiffen slightly as his finger slides inside me, but soon the movement of his tongue on my clit and his finger has me melting into the wrap again. I can feel a tension building inside me. Not fear, it is something different. My fists clench and I pull at the wrap under me, trying to fight the tension that is building in me. His mouth moves faster and faster and suddenly, stars rain down on me as I cry out. I know that I have just had an orgasm; I have heard of it before and the way the pleasure shudders through me has me screaming out in desire.

He chuckles again as he rises up, trailing kisses up my body. He sucks in my nipple and I groan at the pleasure. My eyes flutter at the feeling of new tension building and I wonder if I will orgasm again. I can feel his hardened manhood pressing into my opening and I feel a moment of panic...he is too large to fit.

"It will only hurt for a moment," he says before he returns to licking and suckling my breast.

He moves inside of me and for a moment, it feels like he is pushing against something deep within. Then his cock pushes it aside and he plunges in to the deepest part of me. I scream in pain and I can feel a gush of fluid between my legs. He stops moving and he slides his hand down to my clit where he begins rubbing it. He lies there, bringing that sweet tension back to me as I feel my body adjust to his large size.

As the tension builds, I can't stop myself from moving. I see him grin, his dark eyes sparkling as he starts to move in me slowly. I can feel myself gripping his thick cock each time he pulls out and sucking him back in when he plunges back into my depths. I moan under him and my nails bite into his back, creating fresh wounds on his skin.

As my body begins to shake, his strokes speed up and he starts to slam his cock into me. I buck back, urging him to go deeper and harder with each thrust and he obliges my need. He thrusts hard, once...twice...on the third thrust, I am screaming his name, cheering it like the crowd, "Kadius, oh Kadius, yes, yes...Kad-ius!"

He grunts loudly as he comes, both of us plummeting

over the edge of glory. As the room starts to come back to me, I know that my virgin blood has stained the wrap and I smile as he says, "You are the best trophy this man has ever received."

31 THE STRANGER

The guys were taking me out tonight and I was nervous. I had not been to a club in three months after my big breakup with Karlie. She broke my heart after leaving me for a man that she worked with. Sean was his name, and after meeting him once, I knew how smarmy he was. "He enjoys going out and you don't. Our year together was fun but you're not what I need in a man at this time in my life." Her final words had cut me to the bone.

Sighing, I washed the hairs from my face after shaving and splashed on some aftershave. Josh texted me as I was buttoning up my dark blue Hugo Boss shirt.

"Hurry up, man! We're outside!" his message read. I reluctantly grabbed my wallet and headed out my front door.

I was greeted with a round of applause as I forced my tall frame into the front seat of Josh's black Acura. Don yelled, "It's about time man! Let's get this party started! Wooo!" I laughed and took the beer that Don handed me and shouted, "Cheers!"

Josh knew how upset I had been about Karlie. I could barely get out of bed some days, let alone go to a club. He told me earlier in the week that it was time for me to get over her and realize that what she and I had was over. Our conversation had been a long one and it hit some hard truths that I wasn't ready to face. Karlie had been the love of my life and getting over her was tough. I need this, I thought. It was good to let loose for once in a long time.

My friends had decided to go all out and rent a VIP booth at a new club in town. It was called "Electric" and I could see why. The line to get in was a mile long and snaked past the red velvet ropes. Josh walked straight towards the front booth and stated his name. We were immediately let in, bypassing the line, and were led upstairs to a private booth with leather seats and champagne already chilling in a metal ice bucket.

A pretty waitress approached, popping the cork on the bottle and pouring us each a glass of the bubbly liquid into the crystal glasses. We clinked our glasses together while all five of my friends shouted, "To Brian!" I raised my glass in appreciation and drank it down. The cold liquid gave me a rush of excitement. I had a feeling this was going to be a great night. If I was going to party, I was going to do it right.

We decided it was time for real drinks and headed to the bar downstairs after Don noticed the group of girls dancing on the floor below. They were hot and dancing seductively. I noticed one girl that stood out; she word a body-hugging tube dress in bright white that caused her bronzed skin to stand out. Her large breasts seemed to be swaying to the beat of the music. At the bar, the guys noticed me watching her and begged me to approach her for a dance. I declined their silliness, knowing she was there to have fun with her friends.

I finally got a bartender's attention and asked for a beer. While waiting, I was bumped into by someone. I turned around and it was the girl. She smiled and yelled for a bartender.

"Hey Mickey! Can you get me water, please?" I stared at her and took in the scent of her presence. She smelled like fresh-cut roses. It was almost intoxicating. I smiled back at her and asked if I could buy her a drink.

"Thanks, but maybe later," she said, winking at me while walking away.

My group of friends crowded around me whistling and giving each other a high-five just because I talked to the girl in the white dress. They all turned their attention to the dance floor again. A hot song was spinning and the music started pumping. Josh shouted over the music, "Hey, let's go dance with those girls!" I asked which ones and he shot me a strange look, "The hot ones, man!" We walked towards the floor and started to dance inside their group. I yelled out, "I get the one in white!"

I walked up behind her and danced with her, sliding my hands up and down her arms. She turned and smiled, grinding her ass against my crotch. Oh god, I could feel myself getting hard. I kept at it, hoping that she didn't feel my growing cock moving against her body. The DJ put on a slow sexual song that got my blood pumping. She turned and wrapped her arms around me, pushing herself against me as I rubbed my fingers through her hair. She lifted her head up and looked me in the eyes, her hands moving down to my ass. This was moving fast but I didn't care. Her hands on my body and her large breasts pressing against my chest was more than I could handle, I grabbed her wrists and kissed her neck as she writhed against me.

I spoke into her ear, "Honey, you are driving me crazy. I may have to go stand behind a table to hide how much you turn me on." She threw her head back and laughed. I looked at her long brown throat arched back and could not resist kissing it. She tasted like honey and cinnamon.

She grabbed my fingers and started walking off the dance floor. "Let's get some air," she said as I trailed behind her. She led me to the balcony area and was unsure of what she wanted, but I was hoping it was more than just getting air. I stared at her beautiful ass as she walked me into a room that had a large window overlooking the club.

She winked and murmured, "No one can see us, babe. It's a one-sided mirror. Sexy huh?" Locking the door behind her, she turned on a large fan and walked to a large table in the middle of the room. Her blue eyes sparkled as her hair blew back behind her in waves. She tugged down her dress, exposing her breasts that were showcased by small pink nipples. They stood at attention as she pulled the bottom of her dress up to her hips, exposing her succulent center.

I stepped towards her, wanting so badly to touch her. I bent down and took her left nipple into my mouth, savoring the taste of her, while massaging her right breast and squeezing it ever so gently. She leaned forward and slowly undid my zipper, smiling at me the entire time. Then she lay back onto the table. Her legs opened wide to let my bulging hardness inside her wetness. I bent to kiss her and a high-heel was immediately pressed against my chest stopping me. I slowly removed the heel and placed it over my shoulder while moving her other leg to my other shoulder.

As I slid my cock up and down her wet slit, she moaned. I couldn't take it anymore, I entered her fully. Her pussy was so tight and slick that I wasn't prepared for how good she would feel. I began thrusting all of my cock inside of her; she took it all and reached down to rub her clit, sliding her fingers over my hardness as I moved out of her. Screaming for me to fuck her harder I did.

My entire body was vibrating with intense pleasure and her moaning gave way to shouts of erotic lustiness. I raised my head up just once to see people walking by on the balcony, yet no one noticed us. I drove into her even more as the others couldn't see us, causing her to almost yelp with a mixture of desire and pain, her finger rubbing her clit fast in a circular motion that was making her pant. I could feel her pussy tightening around my shaft as she screamed out in ecstasy. Her shuddering body a signal for me to release all that I had deep inside of her. I came with a vengeance, forgetting everything except for this magical interlude.

As I tried to catch what was left of my breath, the bronzed beauty in the white dress wrapped her legs tightly around my waist, and pulled me down onto her. She leaned up to whisper in my ear, "Let's go dance." She released her legs from my waist and moved out from underneath me. Before I could get myself or my mind put back together, she disappeared out the door.

32 THE WATCHER

I was unsure when my friend called me with the invitation. The tone in her voice was playful yet she knew it would touch a nerve. I was finally invited to the Night Owl, a club that was a preview for sex beyond what most imagined. Ginger, who seemed to have friends in all kinds of high places, pulled some strings and was able to get me a guide to this mysterious club. The owner was a man by the name of Damien.

Getting ready for the night out wasn't painstaking as I knew no one would be seeing me. I chose a simple jean-skirt and a white tee, with sneakers to round out what I thought was appropriate attire. I slowly did my makeup, hoping it would delay the inevitable. I sipped my wine as I curled my long hair into waves down my back, hoping the wine would give me courage for what was ahead of me. While I finished touching up the gloss on my lips, I heard a two quick toots of a car horn outside my apartment; the car was here to take me to this exclusive and very secret location

The driver was a tall brooding man dressed in a black suit. He opened the back door of the Mercedes for me as I approached the vehicle, giving me a small nod of approval. While the driver drove to a faraway place unknown to me, I thought back on why I was even pursuing this adventure. Ginger had maintained that I was sexually repressed and that I must be the only single girl in New York City. "Just think about what you're missing, Liz! I promise, after this experience, you will not be single long," teased Ginger. Thus, the arrangement began. I was nervous yet excited about what the night would bring me.

I finally arrived at what looked like a warehouse, tall and foreboding with a façade of red brick and gothic architecture. Set amongst an unknown forest, it seemed almost abandoned except for the fleet of fancy cars parked in the small drive next to the entrance. The driver helped me out of the car and escorted me into the hulking doors and down a long black hall where Damien stood, waiting.

Damien, a tall man with bright blue eyes and dark curls, looked me up and down; it seemed that he was pulling every nuance of my soul into his smoldering eyes. He smirked at my attire and lightly took my elbow, leading me into the unknown.

The atmosphere was a shock. The outside of the building seemed so dark, yet the inside was reminiscent of a 1950's jazz club. Heavy red velvet drapes graced the windows, and the scent of whiskey and cigars was heavy in the air. The aroma went to my head in a way that I wasn't used to, causing me to feel transported to another era. The slow seductive music drifting throughout the room was entrancing.

Damien stood quietly for a moment, letting me take in the magnetic ambience, and then again, grasped my elbow and led me to a well-lit office. He poured me a glass of wine and I accepted. He slowly gathered papers that were neatly placed upon his desk and slid them towards me. His gaze was heavy upon me as I read the conditions of the agreements and hurriedly signed what could be the experience of a lifetime or one that I would be ready to forget.

My hands were shaking as I slid the papers back to

Damien, all the while feeling his blue eyes burning a hole through my body. He took the papers and swept them into a folder and promptly filed them away while I stared at the dark glossy curls covering his head. There was a small amount of lust starting to shimmer inside myself while staring at his well-chiseled face; the anticipation of what I was about to endure didn't make it any easier, so I downed the entire glass of wine.

He looked at me with intrigue in his eyes and asked if I wanted a refill. I shook my head and just sat there. Finally, he stood and walked around the desk and offered his hand to me. I granted my right hand to him as he helped me up from the plush office chair and led me into a secret door behind his desk. As we walked through, I saw a room with floor to ceiling windows and couches that lined the walls of the small area. I don't pay attention to the surveillance cameras above the door.

He finally spoke. "Where would you like to sit?" It wasn't a hard choice to make as all of the couches were covered with a fine sateen fabric with plump cushions.

"Here in the middle," I said, as he led me to the black sofa.

Damien looked over me as I sat and explained, "Choose one of these three windows. Your time expires when the show you choose expires." He pushed a button that told the other rooms that the Watcher was ready. He hesitated and I smiled nervously and with a curt nod, Damien left the room.

I spoke out loud, "Window one," as it was the first that my nervous mind could think of and immediately the window opened revealing a splayed woman on a table, nude. There was a large muscled man with is head hidden between her legs, lost in her cries of pleasure. I moaned instinctually…her throaty calls for more hit something inside of me that had been hidden for so long. He licked his long tongue up and down her clit, making her tremble and shake with unbridled desire.

I got up and stepped towards the window to get a closer look at this erotic demonstration and noticed the man had his hand wrapped around himself stroking himself hard while licking her hot center. His deft strokes with both his tongue and hand were amazing to behold. His cock was throbbing and I wondered if he would ejaculate on her wetness. I slowly backed away from the window and sat down on the sofa, realizing that my panties were becoming wet. It didn't help that my nipple grazed the sofa as I sat, sending a jolt of electricity through my already pulsating body. I tucked my legs underneath me to prevent something I couldn't control. I can't believe I'm watching this, I thought.

Suddenly, the man stood up, grabbed his shaft and thrust into the woman. Lifting her legs over his shoulders, he pounded into her, grunting and moaning with pleasure. I could see her taking all that he had, the entirety of his largeness pushed firmly inside of her, his balls slapping against her ass. My muscles were blooming with desire deep inside me, making me wetter as seconds ticked by.

Suddenly, the man pulled out of the moaning woman and pushed a button. The table she was on lowered and another man entered the room. He was stroking his hardness and was ready to play. The muscled man went to another table and lay down, waiting for the woman to get on top of him. She threw her right leg over his body, slipped his huge cock inside of her, and started riding him. My panties were soaking wet and I wasn't sure if I could keep my fingers away from my hard nipples.

The second man slowly approached the table where the couple was fucking, his swollen shaft in his hand; he gently touched the woman's ass. He pulled out a bottle of lubricant and rubbed it on the woman's ass, sliding his hardness up and down to get her entrance ready. I shielded my eyes with my hands and then spread my fingers apart. I wasn't sure what I was watching, but I knew I couldn't look away. He pushed a button to raise the table so that he was able to slip inside her at an even angle. He slowly pushed inside her until he was completely in. The woman was engorged with two cocks and my clit was begging for the same.

I couldn't take it anymore. I knew no one could see me, so I reached under my jean skirt to my swollen and wanting bud, slowly rubbing as my breathing increased. The grunts and moans by the threesome were more than I could bear. The man on the table had his large hands around the woman's hips while he pounded her, and I wanted something inside me as well. I pushed my finger inside me, feeling the wetness. It seemed that I was feeling what they were feeling. My finger slid in and out of my wetness, my wrist rubbing against my clit. When their tempo increased, so did mine.

When the threesome reached climax, their orgasms were loud and animalistic and my own orgasm was just as strong. I shouted out in complete satisfaction not worrying if Damien could hear me. I shuddered and slipped my hand out of my panties, the large sofa cushions a relief on my back. My fingers were covered in my juices and the smell in the small room was rife with it.

What seemed to be blinding lights powered into the small room and I blinked, shaking off the mind-blowing orgasm I had just experienced. Reality kicked in for me as I saw Damien's powerful frame standing in the doorway of the now-bright room, his gaze looking right between my legs through to my underwear. I adjusted my clothes as quickly as I could. He walked towards me, desire filling those cerulean blue eyes, and reached for my hand. I stood up, my knees buckling and he turned to grab my waist. Appreciating his strength and taking in his masculine cologne I fall into him. My body clenches at his touch and I feel something deep below start to build back up. Straightening up with torment laced in his eyes like he doesn't want me to leave, he takes my elbow and ushers me towards the door. Reaching out for the doorknob he leans down and his whispers hoarsely into my ear, sending tingling sensations throughout my body "I hope you enjoyed the show as much as I did."

33 THE DOCTOR

He glances at his watch for the hundredth time that day and fights down the sigh. Still, the patient can see that he is impatient and she quickly asks her questions before he leaves her. She can't help but wonder why someone so handsome could look so worried. She takes in his short brown hair, chocolate brown eyes and his square jaw. He could be a model and he was young for a doctor, only 27 from what she heard.

He was one of the most popular OBGYNs around; partly because he was drop dead gorgeous with his swimmer's build – long, lean and athletic, but partly because he was an amazing doctor with an excellent bedside manner. Biting her lip, the patient asks, "Is something wrong Dr. Hunt?"

He glances up at her, a sheepish grin on his lips, "I have been a horrible doctor today, haven't I Mrs. Smith?"

She shakes her head, "No, nothing is wrong. I am simply distracted. An old friend is coming in that I attended medical school with. I haven't seen her in years, although we exchange the occasional email. She's in town for a conference."

Pulling out his wallet, Dr. Hunt slides out a photo. In

the picture is a group of young people in lab coats and he points to an exotic woman with dark black, wavy hair, olive skin and violet eyes. She is petite to his large size and she is gazing up at Dr. Hunt instead of at the person taking the picture. "You make a cute couple," Mrs. Smith says as Dr. Hunt blushes deeper, "When will she be here?"

"In two hours," he says.

"Well, I won't keep you then so your schedule is free by the time she comes in. Be sure to enjoy her while she's here," Mrs. Smith says, her eyes sparkling as she walks out of the room.

****

Two hours later and Dr. Hunt's nerves are raw. The day had gone quickly and thanks to the short talk with Mrs. Smith, he had been able to keep his focus on his patients. Now, however, all he can do is pace back and forth as he closes up the office. He had sent his staff home a half hour earlier and had cleaned himself up.

As he turns off the light in the bathroom, he hears a knock at the front door. Opening it, he smiles at the sight of Chloe, his beautiful Chloe. Blushing at his thoughts, he breathes her in. Her exotic scent is spiced with some unknown flavor and she looks amazing in her black trench coat. Her oversized suitcases are on the floor at her feet.

"You haven't been to the hotel." It isn't a question, more of a statement.

"No, I wanted to see you first. Can you give me a tour?"

Her cheeks are flushed and he fights the urge to check her temperature to make sure she is alright. He can't help the need building inside of him as he takes her through the small office, showing her the waiting rooms, his office, and the exam rooms. Her eyes miss nothing, but her pretty face continues to flush deeper and he wonders if she is sick.

"Carl, you have done well for yourself," Chloe says as they reach an exam room, "I was surprised when you chose your specialty, you have the hands of a surgeon so I always thought you would go that way."

His dark eyes met her violet ones and she almost took a step towards him – the desire beckoned to her and gave her the strength to carry on with her plan. "You inspired me with all your talk about the strength of women and bringing children into the world," he says.

Taking a deep breath, she says, "Well, maybe you can help me...do you find it hot in here," she adjusts her heavy coat, "I haven't been feeling that well."

The doctor rises inside him and he moves to her, taking her delicate wrist in his. A dozen illnesses start flying through his head as he begins to assess her glassy eyes, and the heat emanating from her. He can feel it through her trench coat. "Why don't you take off the coat and I will give you an exam?"

She smiles at him and his nerves dance with anxiety. Taking a step back, her mouth makes a small pout as she unties the trench coat. Allowing it to slide to the ground, Carl bites back the groan that is forming in his throat – she is completely naked except for a pair of garters. And she is as beautiful as he imagined. Her skin is flawless and her small breasts are perky and tight. His eyes slip down to her trim waist and then lower as he sucks in a breath of air, she is completely shaved!

"You see doctor," she purrs, "I have this ache right here." She places her hands on her pelvis, her fingers gently brushing the v between her legs, "It really needs healing."

Excitement courses through him and his cock grows hard as he watches her saunter to the exam table. She jumps onto it and lies down completely, spreading her legs. Her eyes blaze with desire as she says, "I have waited too long for my exam from you. I have missed you so much and I need you to examine me fully, doctor."

Desire shoots through him, right to the tip of his cock and he is overwhelmed by the joy he is feeling. He has wanted her since they were in school together. Walking over, he grasps her wrists when he reaches her and traps them above her head, exposing her breasts to his perusal.

She groans and wiggles her hips in encouragement as he says, "I guess we'll need to start with the breast exam first."

Massaging her breasts, he smiles as she shudders at his touch. His thumbs rub her nipples and he can feel his cock weeping. He has wanted this for so long, he isn't sure if he can control himself long enough. The taste of her is exhilarating and he sucks her nipple into his mouth. She gives a little cry as his teeth gently tug at the nipple and his hands slide over her stomach.

He kneads the flesh and runs his tongue down her stomach, tension pushing him closer and closer to his orgasm as she sighs out his name. He stands up and moves to the end of the table. Pulling out the stirrups, he says, "You're breasts look perfect, no worries there, but I am going to need to do an internal exam. Place your feet inside the stirrups and scoot all the way to the end of the table please."

Her cheeks are flushed with passion as he spreads her legs wide. Leaning between them, he sucks on her nipples as he rubs his bulge against her. She writhes under him, her moans becoming more urgent with every second. He slides down her body and positions his face between her legs. Looking up at her closed eyes and rapturous face, he takes a small lick. She tastes like cinnamon and he groans at the heady scent.

Sucking her clit into his mouth, he slides his finger into her tightness and begins working his mouth and finger in tandem. He can feel her tightening around his finger as she cries out, her orgasm shaking her entire body as she rears up in the stirrups.

Chuckling at the effect he is having on her, he slips his

pants off, his cock springing free and jutting up to his stomach. He runs his hand up the shaft, grinding his teeth at how hard he is – he hopes he doesn't come the minute he enters her. Clearing his throat, he says, "I'm going to do the internal exam now. You are going to feel a bit of pressure as I enter."

She smiles and bites her lip and he slides his cock up and down her slit, wetting it in her juices before he slowly enters her tight, wetness. She bucks up, trying to urge him deeper, but he goes slow, burying himself to the hilt before pulling back out until just the tip is inside.

He rocks his hips and pushes deep inside her. When he is as deep as he can go, he reaches for the stirrups and pushes them farther apart as he pulls her down farther on the table. He thrusts hard into her, his brow furrowing as he concentrates on not coming yet. He can feel her walls sucking him deeper, tightening and then releasing as he works his cock in and out. He thrusts harder and harder, gaining speed as she writhes under him, urging him on.

He reaches between them and rubs her clit as he thrusts and as she starts screaming her release, he feels the tension build up to an unbearable point. His cock bursts and he can feel his hot load coating her insides as it gushes from him. He can feel her clenching around him and he roars as another orgasm rocks him into her a final time.

He collapses on her stomach and he feels her arms wrap around him as she says, "Dr. Hunt...you've healed me."

34 THE INTRUDER

"Okay, darling," I say into the phone, "Don't worry about anything. I'll just eat in and get some writing done."

"You sure," my husband, Ian, says, "I can cancel the drinks with Andie if you want."

I shake my head and realize that he can't see me, "No, really, it's okay. I'm just going to take a shower and write. I'll see you soon."

"Okay, keep my bed warm," he said and I smile even though I feel disappointment that Ian is having drinks with Andie, his VP of operations, again.

Clicking off the phone, I toss it onto my desk and head to the shower. The water is soothing and I stand in it until it begins to run cold. Getting out, I slide on my cotton robe, put on a pair of panties and head into the kitchen to grab a drink. The news is playing on the counter TV and I watch it, listening to the forecast as I take another swallow of my martini. Then I hear a click.

The noise is low and I turn down the TV and listen. I hear another click and it sounds like someone is rattling the knob on the back door. Racing to the door, I flick on the security light and glance out. The pool shimmers in the light, but nothing else moves in the yard. I check the door and see the lock is in place.

Must be my imagination, I chide myself and head back to my office, gathering my drink on my way. I begin typing away, trying to find the thread of my story, but I can't focus. I keep thinking about the back door, wondering if there had been someone out there.

After ten minutes of trying, I give up. There is no way I am going to get any writing done with my imagination running overtime. I flick off the computer and start moving through the house, turning off the lights. As I reach the hallway, a hand reaches out from the darkness, wrapping around my mouth.

Fear lances through me and I feel tears stinging my eyes. I gulp down the panic and kick backwards, feeling a moment of satisfaction when I hear him cry out in pain. I race up the stairs but near the top, he grabs my ankles and I fall to the ground.

He flips me over and I get my first good look at him. I see nothing but dark clothes and a dark mask. His brown eyes are shining with excitement and for some reason; a part of me reacts to that excitement. He pulls my hands up above my head and rips open my robe and that movement jerks me back to reality. I bring my knee up into his groin and break free as he stumbles back away from me.

I run into my bedroom and lock the door behind me. Reaching for the phone, I scream as the door explodes inward and he grabs me. Throwing me onto the bed, I bang my head on the headboard. I see stars and I can barely move as I watch him rummaging through my chest of drawers. He pulls out the stockings and moves towards me. Catching my breath, I scream and shuffle away from him, trying to make it to the bathroom.

He catches me before I do, wrapping one strong arm around my waist. I claw at his arm and flail around, trying to kick him as he tosses me back on the bed. He climbs on top of me and captures my arms in one hand. Winding the stocking around both of my wrists, he ties me to the head board. I struggle against the binds, but the knot is too strong and he has full control over me.

"Stop struggling or I will kill you," he whispers into my ear, "You are going to enjoy what I do to you."

Tears sting my eyes I go completely still. I want to live so I nod my head as fear causes my heart to race. He lifts up off of me and moves until he is straddling my waist. He slides my robe open again and begins to gently massage my breasts. He pinches the nipple slightly and I am disgusted at how my body reacts to his touch. I spit at him and his hands slide up to my neck, gently pressing into it. "Do that again and I will snap your beautiful neck," he growls.

And I believe him. I don't want what he is doing but my only chance of survival is to let him. He reaches down and frees his cock from his pants. My eyes widen at how large it is. Rubbing it, he moves forward until his cock is hovering at my mouth. "Suck it until I'm hard," he says, "And don't even think about biting down or I will kill you slowly and make you regret it."

Tears streaming my cheeks, I open my mouth and allow him to shove his cock inside. I suck him and gag on the salty taste of his juices. He moves his hips, sliding his cock in and out of my mouth. I do nothing but swallow what he has to give me, my lips working on his flesh as he fucks my mouth hard. Each thrust goes down my throat and he begins groaning on top of me. I can't fight the heat spreading through my body at his noises and I feel wetness between my legs.

As he cries out, I feel his seed flood my mouth and I gag on it before I am forced to swallow the hot liquid. He pulls out of my mouth and grins, "That's a good girl. Lick your mouth clean."

I do what he asks, licking every drop of him from my lips and from his cock as he shoves it toward me. He drops to the side of the bed and pulls off his pants. "Let's see if you're wet." He straddles me again, his wet cock dripping onto my stomach as he reaches back and slides his hands into my panties.

His thumb presses down on my clit and guilt washes over me as my body reacts to his touch, my clit throbbing as his thumb works it. He slides his finger deep inside me and I groan trying to stop the desire from spreading. He begins to stroke himself and I close my eyes, "Watch me," he demands.

I open my eyes and watch him as his finger slides in and out. As the tension builds, I squeeze my eyes shut again, trying to stop the orgasm that is building. He growls, "Open them."

But I shake my head and squeeze them tighter as he forces another finger into me. Growling, he rips away my underwear and my eyes fly open in fear. He moves down and tries to push his thigh between my legs, but I keep them shut tight.

He presses his other knee and pushes my legs apart, and then he is driving deep into my center. I scream at the invasion and he places his hands on my mouth to muffle them as he pounds into me. His cock fills me completely and I cry out, arching into this man who is taking me and embarrassed that my body is reacting to it as my orgasm builds.

He snarls again and pulls out. Flipping me over onto my stomach, he pulls my hips up into the air and shoves himself deep into me from behind. He reaches around and begins playing with my clit and I find myself wiggling around, trying to avoid his touch as my orgasm builds.

I feel myself tighten around him and then I am exploding, crying out my grief and my passion as I do. He pumps inside of me, harder and faster until I feel him spilling into me and his moans slowly fading.

He falls to the side of the bed in exhaustion and I wipe away my tears in the pillow as I hear him ask, "Same place and time next week?"

I glance over at him and giggle, "Hello darling, yes

same place and time..." I pause for a moment to catch my breath, "But only after you fix our bedroom door."

35 THE STRIPPER

I was meeting the guys at Private, a new strip club that opened that week and I was running late. It was another late day at the office and I was more than ready to relax and unwind. It was my birthday after all and it was time to celebrate. I didn't have time to go home and change, so the boys started heckling me about my business suit as soon as I walked in. To shut them up, I bought the next round. We made our way to the private half circle booth in front and settled in.

That's when the music started and she came on.

Her hair was thick and long and she had the toned body of an athlete. She was hard and tight everywhere. Her calf muscles and thighs were defined and toned to perfection. Her waist was small and her breasts were fake. Round, full D-cups that defied gravity where they sat mounted on her chest. Her ass was equally rounded and firm and by the way she danced she knew how to use it. She didn't wear a lot of makeup. As fine as she was physically, it was her mouth and those large, soft lips that hypnotized me.

There was something about the way she was dancing that turned me on instantly. The song was fast and loud, but she was dancing slowly with a gyrating rhythm in between the beats.

Since we were at the VIP booth down in front of the stage it was customary for the dancers to dance right in front of us. The whole time I sat back and watched her and she watched me. She came down front and started dancing in front of my friend opposite of me. He leaned up and whispered something in her ear, but he moved his attention to her breasts, so he didn't notice that she stared deep into my eyes the entire time. When she came to my friend that was in the middle she did it again. It was like she was dancing in front of them, but just for me and I was getting hard just at the thought.

Before she could get to my side, the song ended and she went backstage. I was extremely disappointed, but I knew that she would be out on the floor shortly giving lap dances.

I was wrong. Another dancer came on the stage and then another and still no sight of her. The other girls were hot too, but something about the way *she* stared at me and the memory of those lips kept me distracted. I couldn't get her out of my mind, so I got up to look for her. I told my friends that I was going to the bathroom and I'd be back.

The room was dark and smoky as I made my way around. I acted like I was waiting at the bar for a drink. It was a good excuse for me to look around and see everyone in the club.

I didn't see her at first, but I felt her. I felt her heat slide up behind me and then she whispered, "Hello" seductively into my ear. I didn't turn around immediately because I wanted to play it cool. Inside, my heart was racing.

I motioned the bar tender over for another drink when she leaned in again.

"Follow me," she said.

I turned around and watched her walk through a set of curtains labeled "Red Rooms." I retrieved my beer and nonchalantly strolled through the curtains. There were four doors and only one was slightly open. I entered the room and from the darkness I heard the soft command.

"Sit down."

The walls were carpeted in thick velvet curtains and a single wooden chair stood in the center of the room. There was soft music playing in the background. It was so different and so quiet from the rest of the club I felt like I had stepped into another world.

I sat down, as commanded. My whole body tensed when she appeared from behind the curtain to lock the door. It was dark, but I could see that all she had on was a pair of red panties. I grew hard instantly. She walked toward me, slowly pushing her long hair away from her chest to reveal two perfectly round breasts. Her nipples were puckered and hard. She didn't say anything as she walked behind me pushed a button to lean the chair back and slowly slipped my suit jacket off my shoulders, half way down the back of the chair. I was trapped at the torso – I couldn't move my arms.

It took a minute to get my excitement under control. I was so turned on. Still touching my shoulder she walked around to face me and straddled my lap. She was running her hands across my chest and began undoing my tie when she swiveled her hips on top of me.

"I see you are ready." When I went to answer her she put her finger against those beautiful lips and shushed me. I was disappointed when she got up to move behind me again while dragging my tie away from my neck. I felt her bend down and begin tying my wrists.

"Do not speak and do not touch."

This couldn't be happening. My mind may have had trouble believing it, but my body was ready.

She came back around and straddled me again. Slowly, she began unbuttoning my shirt. When she reached the last button she opened it wide and pushed it back over my shoulders. She ran her long nails down my chest and over my stomach while my nether regions screamed for her touch. She leaned in and kissed my neck. I let out a little moan and that must have pleased her, because she bent down even further to take one of my nipples into her mouth. She did this a few more times; each time switching sides. When she would lean in to kiss my neck, I would feel her hard nipples rubbing against my chest. When she bent down to taste my nipples, I could see more of her perfectly firm backside.

Just when I thought I couldn't take it anymore, she got up and kneeled in from of me. I recovered from her absence fairly quickly when I felt her hands start to unbutton my pants. When she finally succeeds with getting my zipper down, she shimmied my pants and underwear down to my ankles. My cock was hard and exposed. I was ready for the taking. I wanted to touch her so bad. I wanted to make her feel as good as she was making me feel and I wanted to tell her how beautiful she was, but I didn't. I didn't dare risk screwing this up by not following her directions.

She got up and leaned into my face studying my reaction and I could see those luscious lips. It took everything I had not to lean forward and kiss her, but I didn't. I waited. Gently, she pressed her luscious lips into mine. She kissed me so deep and soft and with a desperate need for release that matched mine.

"Don't move." When I looked her in the eyes and she was convinced I wouldn't move, she slowly straddled my body once more. When she leaned in to kiss me again, she lowered herself down just enough to insert the head of my cock, teasing me as she moved her hips rhythmically to the music. Then she lowered herself up and down just enough to play with the tip. It was driving me crazy and my head was spinning from the need to ram myself into her deep and hard.

When she knew that I was suffering, she eased down onto me completely. She was so hot and wet inside that I almost came. She didn't move for a few seconds while she nibbled at my ear. It sounded like she was whispering something in Spanish, but I couldn't make it out.

She started to move again in rhythm to the music in the background. Each time she lowered herself onto me she took all of me in. As the music hit a faster pace so did she. Up and down. Up and down. She began to ride me violently and hard like she couldn't get enough. I didn't move, I just felt. I felt every bit of her each time she raised up to my very tip to when she would smash down again, burying me deep inside her wet passage. She knew how to ride me as if it was me actually doing the thrusting and I was hypnotized.

I was so close and when she started moaning, I knew she was close too. She started going up and down and then grinding at the end of each thrust. Drive after drive she moaned louder and louder and when she went quiet, I knew it was time for us to come together. A few more quick hard thrusts down and I felt my balls tightening. My cock twitched inside her as she continued to ride me. Finally, release came as I spurted inside her, groaning loudly. Lost in the throes of her own shuddering orgasm, she screamed something in Spanish. While I was still inside her she caught her breath and leaned against my shoulder. Then she leaned up and whispered on my lips, "Happy birthday from your friends."

36 THE DEAN

"Mr. Radner, will see you now," the secretary's clipped voice made me roll my eyes. She was an older woman, thin with gray hair and gray glasses, and a nose that she looked down at everyone with.

I knew why I was here and I was excited to get it done. My psych professor had told everyone I had hit on him but it was the opposite. He offered me an amazing grade in exchange for a little heavy petting. I turned him down and he launched a complaint against me out of fear I would file one against him first. Grinding my teeth in frustration, I pushed open the heavy wooden doors to the Dean's office. It was tastefully decorated with heavy black leather chairs, a dark mahogany desk and dark wood book shelves filled to overflowing with books.

I smiled at the sight of it. Men who read were extremely sexy to me and the Dean was no exception. The man was intimidating to most but I loved his salt and peppered black hair and his hard, square jaw. His silver eyes sparkled with intelligence and his smooth, deep voice turned my insides to jelly. If I was going to be accused of sexual harassment, it would have been towards this man, not my puny psych professor.

Crossing the room, I felt his secretary behind me. "Ms. Amanda Adams is here to see you, sir. If there isn't anything else, I will be leaving for the day."

Dr. John Radner looked up from the report on his desk and shot me a scowl before turning a smile toward his secretary. "No, that's all. You have a good weekend Betty."

"Please have a seat Ms. Adams," he said as the door clicked shut behind me.

I moved to the chair across from his huge desk and perched in it, my knees together, my skirt smoothed over my lap and my chin up in defiance. He ignored me as he continued to read the report and I felt my agitation flare. Who the hell does he think he is? I snarl in my head. There is no reason to make me wait.

Shifting in my seat, I catch him staring at me and I grin inwardly. "Now, Ms. Adams, you know why you are here I am sure."

Nodding my head, I say, "I have been accused of a sexual impropriety."

"Yes, quite right." His voice was dry and I could see distaste on his face. "As you can imagine, I need to resolve this quickly and I need to weigh whether you should be expelled."

My mouth dropped. I wasn't expecting him to be so blunt, "Look, I did not try to seduce professor creepy. He came on to me. Offered me an A if I stroked him off..."

"I do not need the dirty details Ms. Adams," he barked, cutting me off, "I have many doubts as to the validity of your words. Professor Kavaliery has been a professor here for ten years and in that time, we have never had a complaint..."

"Probably because the girls sucked him off for their grade," I snarled back, heat flushed my cheeks, but it wasn't from guilt. I was insulted that he thought I would offer up to a creep like Professor Kavaliery.

"That is enough young lady," he barked in reply, "It is

not uncommon for female, and even male, students to proposition a professor for a better grade."

"But why would I," I interject, "I am an honor student. My grades are not threatened in any way and my average for psych has been ninety-eight percent. It seems stupid to risk my scholarship when even failing one test wouldn't drop my grade enough to matter."

His eyes narrowed and I could see the doubt creeping into his eyes. He knows I'm innocent! "Look, Ms. Adams. Either you confess to what you did, or I will have no choice but to revoke your scholarship and expel you."

"You will not!" I yell, jumping from my seat. I round the desk, fury urging me on. I turn his chair and placing my hands on either armrest, I lean into him. The heat from my anger set my blue eyes blazing and I can feel the heat pool in my stomach, my body aching from a combination of my attraction for the Dean and my anger. "Let me say this again...I...did not...try to...seduce..."

The door flies open as a man, his nose buried in a book, rushes through the door. Panic rushes through me and I realize that I look like I am about to climb into the Dean's lap. Instead of stepping back, I drop down onto the floor and shuffle under the large desk. The Dean gives me a startled look and then pulls his chair under the desk in frenzy. I look around, just waiting. Even with his legs taking up part of the space, I notice there is still enough room under the desk for a twin sized bed. Why did I drop down? Now I look guilty. I'm such an idiot.

I peek out from under the desk but all I can see are the feet of the professor. "Oh, thank goodness you are alone! I am sorry to barge in but I had a question concerning the policies in the administration's memo. Do you have a minute to go over it?"

"Well, actually, I was just about to leave."

"Really? It won't take more than five minutes."

I felt his sigh as I leaned against his legs trying to listen, "Alright Mr. Read, five minutes and then I really have to leave."

I could hear Mr. Read's reply, but I tuned him out and began to think about my predicament. I hadn't expected him to believe the professor over me. I thought he would realize that I was innocent. My stomach dropped out from under me at the thought of losing my scholarship. With this kind of harassment on my file, I would never get into another college. The bastard was ruining my life.

Fury filled my empty stomach and I fought back the tears. I was going to be expelled because I sexually harassed a professor...and I wasn't even guilty. I stared at the Dean's crotch – I could make out the large bulge of his cock. Even though rage filled me, I had to admit that I had wanted the Dean since I first met him. If I was going to be expelled for sexual impropriety, I might as well make it true.

Reaching out, I cupped the bulge in his pants, smiling as he jerked at my touch. I waited for him to bat my hand away, but after a minute, I realized he was letting me cup him. Smiling, I pressed against his bulge, massaging his growing hardness through his pants.

Not satisfied with the partial reactions I am getting from him, because he is definitely concentrating on what Mr. Read is saying, I slowly unzip his pants and maneuver his manhood out. He is nervously slapping at my hands now and trying not to make too much movement to reveal my existence. I silently laugh and suck in a deep breath at his size. The mushroom head looked bulbous and the sleek, erect shaft was long and thick. I smiled in victory; there was no way he could stand up now.

I stroked the length of him and ran my fingernail across the tip. I felt him tense as my mouth watered. Rising up onto my knees, I licked the saltiness from the tip of his head. A small groan escaped from him and I smiled in another victory. "Are you alright sir?"

"Yes, just a tickle in my throat," I heard him explain. "Are you about finished Mr. Read, I have to..." his voice cracked, "go soon."

Smiling around his cock, I graze my teeth along his shaft taking little nibbles as I do, almost laughing as his shaft jerks in excitement. I suck along his tip, drinking in his uncomfortableness before I slide my mouth over the length of him. I take him as deep as I can and I am surprised that there is still a handful for me to stroke from base to my mouth. I work my hand and mouth in tandem and feel him shuddering under me. I am vaguely aware of the answers he is giving Mr. Read.

The heat between my legs grows and I slip my hand up my skirt and into my panties. My orgasm is so close and I find it so hot to hear the Dean talking academics while I suck him off. I feel like I have complete control of the man pulsing in my mouth.

Flicking my clit with my finger, I flick the tip of his head with my mouth. I imagine him filling me as I rub my slit, first one finger, then another and then a third sliding inside of me. Not able to help myself, I mew around his shaft and hear him groan softly in response.

"Well, I think that is it," I hear Mr. Read finish, "Thank you for your time Dr. Radner."

"Any time Mr. Read, my door is always open," he says and I can hear Mr. Read retreating to the door.

I suck harder, rubbing my clit faster, feeling my orgasm about to explode and I am sure that the Dean is almost there too. The door clicks shut and the Dean pushes me off of him, I groan in frustration but he pulls me out from under the desk, turns me around so I am bent over the cool mahogany and he roughly pushes me down onto it.

Ripping my panties away, he lifts up my skirt and before I can even catch my breath, he thrusts hard into my wetness. I moan in pleasure and rock back...once...twice...three times. My eyes flutter under the pleasure he is driving into me, while my fingers give attention to my engorged clit. On the fourth thrust, we are both crying out and I can feel his release coating my insides as he empties into me while my spasms milk his shaft

He collapses back into his chair and I turn around grinning. Leaning towards him, I pull my skirt down, pick up my ripped panties and I trap him into his chair by grasping his armrests again. I lean closer and kiss his ear, putting my ripped panties into his jacket pocket before I moan in satisfaction, "I guess now I have something to confess Dean Radner. Would you like me to submit a written confession?"

Seeing the challenge in my eyes, he smiles and says, "No, I think we have resolved this issue."

I smile back in victory and turn to walk out. When I reach the door I turn around as he orders, "Oh, Ms. Adams? You're shorthand needs work. I'll see you in my office at the same time tomorrow so we can improve your studies."

Licking my lips and blowing him a kiss I say, "Fuck yeah, you will."

Book of Fantasies Trilogy

COMING SOON!

RED - Book II

BOOK OF FANTASIES

RED

K

ABOUT THE AUTHOR

K is a writer who doesn't write to impress the proper usage of words taught by English Professors everywhere. Rather, K writes to elicit usage of imagination and feelings experienced by all mankind worldwide. K writes for the adventurer, the romantic, and the secret curiosity hidden in all of us.